THE SNOW QUEEN
Women of the Wilderness, Book 2
by
Florence Witkop

Published by Forget Me Not Romances, a division of Winged Publications

ISBN: 978-1-947523-80-7

Dear Reader:

This is a book about finding love in the wilderness. My hero and heroine are normal, well-adjusted people. No 'big problems' to overcome, 'horrible childhoods' to deal with or 'angst' to get past. Just nice, every-day people who aren't looking for love but find it in spite of themselves in the forests of northern Minnesota. This particular story takes place during a winter storm and then follows what happens afterwards.

Here's a bit about *The Snow Queen*. When you finish reading this book, if you'll take the time to post a review on Amazon, I'll be forever grateful! Just go to Amazon, type in The Snow Queen by Florence Witkop, and follow the prompts to post your review.

Now, here's what *The Snow Queen* is about:
Two days.
Longer and they'll run out of food – and starve.
If they leave, the blizzard may take them quicker.
What to do? How to survive?
Two people are stranded in the wilderness in a blizzard. They must make a decision while there's still time.
Jase's bad leg complicates everything but Laurie's secret knowledge may save them. If it's for real.
Once they decide on a course of action and carry it out, what will happen?
If they survive, what about the future?
Read this story and fall in love with the north woods in

winter with all its beauty and danger, to pray for two people dealing with the awesome but uncaring forest and, if they survive, to cheer for what happens next.

So now you know a bit about *The Snow Queen*. If you'd like to learn more about my journey as a writer, about the books and short stories I've authored, or learn my thoughts on writing fiction, check out my website at
http://www.FlorenceWitkop.com

Again, thanks for purchasing *The Snow Queen*.

Florence Witkop

CHAPTER 1

It started with the blizzard. The one that came too soon.

The weather channel predicted its arrival for Wednesday evening which, if it had waited until then, allowed plenty of time for people on holiday to enjoy a slow, comfortable, end-of-the-year vacation in cabins scattered about the forest or along the shores of the many lakes in the area and still get home long before the weather turned nasty.

The weatherman, in his honey-smooth voice, said it looked like it would happen exactly as predicted which, he reminded listeners, wasn't always the case. But he was completely sure it would arrive on schedule because there was nothing to mess up his forecast. No sneaky up-flowing weather systems from the south, no zigzags in the jet stream, not a single thing to make the onset of bad weather difficult to predict. So Wednesday evening it would be.

The thing was, the blizzard didn't listen to the weatherman, didn't care what plans mere mortals made, didn't pay attention to those humans scurrying about the northern tier of states as they enjoyed their end-of-the-year holidays while winter, unbeknownst to them, gathered strength and prepared to get nasty and send snow everywhere.

Lots of snow.

Those families who wanted to make their winter vacation last as long as possible watched the news so as to know the last possible moment to leave and still have a safe trip home. Many left on Sunday, allowing three days wiggle room, and most of the rest headed out early Monday morning, which still gave them two days to get home before the big snow arrived. Plenty of time.

Or so they thought.

Only a few people were still in their cabins that Monday evening when the blizzard arrived a full two days ahead of schedule. Less than a few people. Almost none. Just one person, actually.

Me.

My name is Laurie.

CHAPTER 2

It was cold, the kind of cold that stays close to the ground and is one with the snow. I pulled my parka close and pulled the sleeves down as far as possible until they covered my hands. Lucky for me I don't have long arms or my hands would be popsicles but as it was, the sleeves were long enough that I could ignore the gloves I'd brought, stuffing them into the generous pockets of my huge parka, and then I could hold the charcoal between bare fingers as I sketched the cardinal on the Jack Pine branch not too far above me that would eventually be enshrined in another painting of the forest.

That painting, along with others like it, would become part of my portfolio and, as I pictured my future paintings, I also tried to figure how much time I'd have to fill my sketchbook completely. If I left the family cabin tomorrow, Tuesday, or even if I stuck around until Wednesday and got out early enough, before the blizzard hit because it wouldn't arrive until evening, then I'd have time to watch that flash of red streak through the trees enough times that I'd have its flight figured out and could replicate it on canvas.

Yep, that would work. I'd leave Wednesday

morning if I could convince the cardinal to stick around and model for me. If it did, then when I left, if I got out any time before noon, my sketchbook would be brimming with the promise of pictures. Wednesday would be perfect.

As I watched, I had a cunning idea. Maybe I wouldn't have to wait until Wednesday because tomorrow, Tuesday, when I came back to this clump of Jack Pine to continue sketching, I could scatter bread crumbs on the snow to entice him because I really wanted that cardinal and perhaps it would come as soon as it saw food. I could see the picture now, a bright red streak against the green, black, and white of the forest in winter.

As I thought, I realized that it all depended on breadcrumbs. Did Cardinals like breadcrumbs? I didn't know, but I hoped so and that a few scattered on the ground would bring it back and, if I was lucky, even lure other winter birds in.

That extra time would be all it would take to memorialize the forest in winter. My parents had already left, but I had my own car, a tiny city thing, but the roads were plowed and had been as clear as in the summer on the way to the cabin, so the drive home should be equally easy. Besides I'd leave while it was still daylight so I could see any possible icy spots and slow down.

Once every page in my sketchbook was filled, including the margins, which would be done easily before Wednesday afternoon, I'd return to Minneapolis and call my folks to let them know that, yes, I'd put water on the fire in the wood-burning stove so it couldn't possibly set the cabin ablaze and no windows were left open and the refrigerator was empty with the door left open so it wouldn't turn musty. In other words, they could stop worrying. My parents are nice but they worry. A lot.

Having so decided, I forgot time and let my hands move rapidly across the paper until the cardinal flew to another branch and then, after circling a few times during which I simply stared at the bright red against the green pine needles, the black tree trunks, and the pristine white snow that was a light cover in most areas and inches deep in some places, it disappeared.

I'd get more sketches tomorrow, but even if the cardinal didn't return, I had enough that my agent would be happy, as happy as he was capable of being, which was slightly happier than totally miserable, and whether he knew how to smile was debatable, but he was the only agent who'd shown interest in my pictures when I started my life as a professional artist, and we now had a semi-decent relationship. Most of the time.

I imagined his reaction to my new pictures. There might be an entire show of pictures of this lovely, pristine winter with the cardinal picture anchoring the whole thing. Might be? Forget the 'might.' There definitely would be. My ability as an artist grew with each passing year, and few artists make a living from their art, but I manage.

I show storms barreling through the tops of trees that grow so close together and so tall that almost no light penetrates to the floor below and I get that across in my art. Sometimes I show the brooding depths of the dark and fecund forest floor. In other pictures, I show tiny wildflowers growing between the roots of trees, blossoms so small that few people notice them, but I do, and my pictures show how lovely they are, and that's what makes me able to support myself with my painting. I pay the bills with pictures of the north woods. Okay, I barely pay the bills, but I do pay them.

I make no pretense of being a great artist. I simply know and love the forest and have ever since I was a kid playing my solitary games beside the family cabin in the woods, and that love shows in the childish pictures I drew then and the more mature ones I create now.

But time was passing. I'd best stop reminiscing about life and art because the cardinal was gone and tomorrow was another day. And, oddly enough, a few snowflakes were drifting down through the thick canopy of evergreens. The blizzard wasn't due for another couple of days, so thank goodness the flakes had nothing to do with the coming storm. They were just snowflakes, and snow goes hand in hand with winter, so I shouldn't be surprised to see a few now and then.

As I watched, though, more of the white stuff fell through the canopy and grew thicker and thicker as I watched. A snow flurry, I hoped, one of those things that resembles a blizzard but only lasts a few minutes. Nothing important.

Still, even with the snow flurry that was no more than a nuisance, daylight was waning fast, so I'd be smart to get back to the cabin and settle in for the evening and then for the night. Sighing, I closed my sketchbook, stuck my charcoal in one of the capacious pockets of my parka and headed back to the cabin while reminding myself to remember bread crumbs the next morning that would hopefully lure the cardinal back with his entire family in tow.

Maybe I could put some in a bag when I reached the cabin and return to scatter them before it grew dark? I glanced upwards at the darkening sky and decided that wouldn't happen, even though the snow flurry had ended as I'd expected.

By the time I was in the cabin and had thrown wood on the fire in the black stove that kept the place warm and had turned to fixing something to eat, there'd been several more snow flurries. More than was usual and there was a bit of snow accumulating on the ground beneath those huge evergreens, but nothing scary.

If they continued, I decided, there'd be a thin layer of snow on top of what had already been there when we arrived before Christmas. It would be pretty and was good reason to wait for the morning to toss breadcrumbs everywhere because, if I did it tonight, they might be covered by snow in the morning. When I checked, I discovered that there wasn't much bread left, so I decided against a sandwich because the last loaf was almost gone, and I wanted those remaining slices for cardinal bait.

I checked the cupboards and figured that the few items in it would get me through another day or two. No reason to head for a town that was almost fifty miles away for more supplies. So I gathered what was already in the refrigerator and had been opened and so had to be either eaten or tossed, and I somehow turned it all into a unique casserole that, even though it was a bit unusual given the ingredients, tasted okay and was too much food for one meal but could become breakfast the next day if I was willing to eat leftovers when I got up. Which I was.

So I had dinner and washed the dishes and put them away and then cleared off the table and covered it with my sketches that I examined by the light of an oil lamp because we've never had electricity at the cabin, choosing gas for the refrigerator and stove and oil for light. Visitors called it primitive and seldom returned.

I made a few additions to the sketches from memory and imagination, but was fairly satisfied with what covered the table so, as the old-fashioned wind-up clock on the wall said it was nearing midnight, I swept all the sketches back into the folder that I carry almost everywhere and put it on the shelf where it would be ready for me in the morning.

And jumped when a knock came at the door.

No one should be at the end of the road in the depth of the forest knocking at the door of a normally unoccupied cabin at midnight. No one should be on the other side of the door.

We usually spent the holidays with family but this year all of our relations had gone to southern climes, so we'd decided to go somewhere too, only we went north, and no friends wanted to be with us badly enough to rough it without electricity, so the person on the other side of the door wasn't family or friends.

Who was it?

The thing is, the forest isn't normally filled with dangerous people, and when someone knocks we answer because it's the neighborly thing to do.

So I opened the door to a man about my age, maybe a bit older, who stared at me from darkish eyes, some unknowable shade of a possible brown but perhaps dark blue, in an absolutely normal male face framed by a parka similar to my own but he also wore ultra-warm pants and huge, clunky snowmobile boots. A pair of large double mittens were held in one hand as the other was raised to knock again.

The face spoke. "I saw the light and hoped someone was home."

I looked beyond him for a vehicle but saw none and had heard none arrive. Of course not, those clunky boots would make driving a car impossible. No way to step on the gas or brake. "How'd you get here?"

His face went somewhat grim. "I started my jaunt on a snowmobile. But I walked the last few miles. Through snow."

"Because it broke down?" He nodded.

Again, I looked past him but it was too dark to see much of anything, so it was impossible to know if there were tracks in the driveway. Then my gaze swerved aside, and I saw the trail of boot prints that were barely visible in the snow of the open ground between the cabin and the forest. They paralleled my own tracks that were now so faint as to be almost buried beneath the snow flurries that had flirted with the small clearing where the cabin sat. Even now snow fell, another flurry consisting of huge flakes that were almost invisible in the dark. More snow than I'd expected. I was surprised. "You came through the forest?"

"Yep, and it wasn't easy going." He indicated the two sets of tracks. "I'm glad I ran across your tracks back there or I could be in a heap of trouble right about now. But I did see them, and they were fresh enough that I figured if I followed them, I'd find someone. Some place to spend the night. To be safe."

He looked straight at me to acknowledge that it was asking a lot to allow a perfect stranger to spend the night. "It's very late, and the snow is coming down hard." Yes, it was. As I looked, I realized that it was coming down harder than when I'd been outside earlier. Much harder.

After a pause, during which I stared from him to the snow that was on the ground and in the air and seemed to be falling faster and faster as I watched, he said grimly, "The blizzard has arrived."

My breath went out in a whoosh and my eyes went wide. My tiny car sat in the driveway and, now that my eyes were adjusted enough to the dark to see somewhat clearly, I checked it out and, with a sinking heart, realized that it was almost lost beneath what seemed like a ton of snow that must have fallen while I was inside and warm.

What would I do if he was right? Could the blizzard actually have arrived? How would I get home? My tiny car wouldn't manage a mile in that much snow. "It can't be here. Can't be."

He stood without moving, not coming into the cabin until he was sure that his company would be okay, as he said, "That's what I thought when my snowmobile broke down and I was miles from anywhere. That I had lots of time to figure out what to do. Then the snow started falling and, when it didn't stop, I knew I could be in a world of hurt."

What I'd thought were snow flurries were the beginning of the blizzard, coming in fits and starts before settling down to a steady snowfall.

He'd been alone in the forest as a blizzard began and had, by some miracle, found what was likely the only safe place in a hundred miles and yet he stayed on the porch because it was my cabin and he had manners.

I backed quickly and ushered him inside, but he stood there unmoving, not wanting me to get the wrong idea as the dark beyond his back grew even darker and the night even scarier. I said, "I can't drive you anywhere. Not now, anyway, in the dark. My car can't be trusted in a storm."

He nodded that he understood, and we stared at one another in silence as the snow filtering through the trees came down even harder.

I would trust him to be a decent person. It's what I'd want if I were stranded in the forest in a blizzard. "Come in. Please."

"Will your car get us out of here in the morning?"

My expression said I didn't know, that I didn't want the blizzard to be here, didn't want it to be happening, didn't want to think about storms. "The forecast said the blizzard will start Wednesday evening and the forecaster was so sure about the timing."

The snow I was looking at said otherwise. "Maybe this is just a precursor to the real storm?" I sounded hopeful but my words were hardly more than a frightened whisper. "If so, tomorrow should be good and we'll manage if I drive carefully. I'll bring a shovel in case we get stuck."

I wanted to believe my own words, so I repeated them, louder this time. "Perhaps this is just a flurry. Must be a flurry." But even I heard the alarm in my voice.

His voice, on the other side of the threshold, was grim. "What I walked through wasn't a flurry. The forecast was wrong." He swept an arm to take in the small space of the outside world visible from the doorway and then, as if thinking that I might need more convincing, he stepped to one side so I could see the whole clearing where the family cabin stood in order to better see the snow coming down thick and hard. Inches were accumulating as we watched. "See for yourself."

CHAPTER 3

I looked hard at the outside world and he was right. As I peered into a dark that was now so complete that only the backdrop of freshly fallen white snow allowed me to make out anything, I saw that my tracks had completely filled in while we talked and his were quickly disappearing. I thought about his trek to the cabin. "If you'd taken longer to get here, the trail would have gone cold."

He nodded grimly. "Someone was watching over me." And then, as a gust of wind that managed to somehow penetrate the thick trees sent snow cartwheeling everywhere and caused a white-out, he accepted my invitation and stepped inside and closed the door hard, after which we just stared at each other in the dim light of the oil lamp.

He looked around. "Nice cabin and thank you for giving me refuge." He shook himself and began removing his thick, warm outer wear. "It's warm in here. Homey. Comfortable and I can sleep on the floor or anywhere."

"Not necessary. We have a loft with beds." Two lofts, actually, one on each end of the cabin, the larger one for my parents and the small one for me and mine still had the lovely, pink bedspread from my childhood and spread across the floor was the same threadbare rug with teddy bears dancing across it that I'd loved as a child that was now so thin the floor could be seen through it, but I'd repeatedly refused to replace it until actual holes appeared. Which would happen soon.

After those few sentences, we ran out of things to say, so we stared at each other until I noticed him sniff the air that was still filled with dinner and realized with a cringe that he probably hadn't eaten in a long time. "I have lots of food left if you're hungry."

Of course he was hungry, but I didn't know another way to put it because I'm occasionally socially inept, which is part of the reason my agent and I don't always get along. He thinks I should paste on a phony smile and shake hands with everyone and come up with artsy-sounding descriptions of my pictures every time a potential buyer comes near. I grope for words and his eyes roll, but enough customers buy my works that he's semi-happy, though he'd prefer that I was more of an artsy type person who would make him truly rich.

"I'd love something to eat." My unexpected guest's expression said how hungry he was while trying to hide that fact and I almost ran to the refrigerator to re-heat the casserole that wasn't your normal dinner fare but would fill an empty belly.

Unless – Oh dear--

Was he a gourmet? Maybe I should warn him. "It's –" How to describe a mish-mash of leftover everything? Is there a name? "It's whatever was in the refrigerator thrown together and heated up." I flushed. "I won't be insulted if you don't want it." But what else could he eat?

Inspiration struck. "I have peanut butter and jelly." Of course, that would mean using the bread I was saving for Cardinal bait, but if the weather was as bad as it seemed --and it was -- the chances of returning to the forest to finish sketches were growing slimmer by the hour.

"Whatever you have will be fine." He sniffed again. "It smells wonderful."

"Which means you must be starved."

He flushed. "Nothing since breakfast, but I'm sure that whatever you made will be – wonderful." And half an hour later, judging by the way he shoveled the last of the left-over hot dish into his belly and sighed in contentment because he couldn't manage another bite, he actually liked it. Or else he was on the verge of starvation.

We washed the few dishes side by side, him washing and me drying and putting things away, then, as if by mutual, silent agreement, we adjourned, me to the couch and he to the cushiony chair near the wood stove. He dropped into it and stuck his legs out, flexing them in the warmth from the fire. And sighed in contentment once more. And closed his eyes, then opened them as if realizing that it wasn't good manners to fall asleep in front of your hostess.

In that brief moment, though, while his eyes were closed, I'd examined him. Tallish, maybe six feet, with a complexion browned by being outside summer and winter, sandy hair and, though his eyes were closed, I remembered their deep, dark depths. Nice eyes. Friendly. And thoughtful, concerned about something, though I wasn't sure I wanted to know what was on his mind in case it was the blizzard and the dangers it presented.

When he opened them and flushed in embarrassment at being caught napping, I couldn't avoid saying, "I wonder how long the blizzard will last." Then I shrugged off any concern because I didn't want him to think I was a coward, but also because I wasn't ready to deal with the problems inherent in being stranded in a remote wilderness cabin in a blizzard. "It's an inconvenience. The weatherman said two to three days." Which was how long most blizzards last. No big deal. Or so I said without speaking out loud.

He wasn't sure I was right about the storm's duration. "It was predicted to start two days from now. So does the early start mean two additional days of snow and wind?" He shook his head and shuddered a bit and then, as if not wanting to be negative, he smiled, though a bit wanly. "If so, I'm doubly glad I found your place. I'd hate to be stranded in the forest for a week." He took a deep breath and let it out slowly. "I'd maybe survive but it wouldn't be pleasant."

"Plus, you'd have to contend with the drop in temperature that follows a storm."

He shivered. "It'll get really cold when the blizzard ends. It always does." He peered into the hot stove and rubbed his hands to gather more heat. "Lots of degrees below zero."

I hadn't seriously thought about what happens during a blizzard. I'd lived in the north all my life but this particular storm was all wrong and I wasn't prepared. It wasn't supposed to happen until I was safe at home.

Nor had I considered the weather that follows

because I hadn't expected to have to deal with that, either. Now I did and all because this stranger knocked on my door in the middle of the night and showed me what was happening.

Weather filled my mind. Crowded out everything else. Bothered me so much that I wished he'd not come like some mystery man through the snow. "I hope it's over quickly and we can be out of here."

I didn't say that the cabin wasn't provisioned for extended winter stays and that my parents and I had just about exhausted all supplies of every kind during our impromptu winter vacation. But my eyes strayed to the window beyond which was the dangerously low pile of firewood. Another day's worth at the most.

I thought about the almost bare cupboards and almost empty refrigerator. And the fact that there was no cell service and no one knew where I was except my parents and they were used to not hearing from me for days at a time. Sometimes weeks. But I didn't say anything because what good would it do? Why scare my guest?

We watched the fire in silence, each thinking our own thoughts, but oddly, the uncomfortable part of getting to know someone was gone and the silence became companionable, which surprised me because on those few times we'd had company at the cabin, any silence had been strained as guests sought for something to say that didn't include the lack of electricity or plumbing or cell service.

This man, all light brown skin and hair and darker eyes and legs that skimmed the floor and left shadows twice as long as they were seemed to belong to the night, the fire and the flickering light of the oil lamp and the sturdy log walls between us and the blizzard that was just beginning to roar through the north country and how a person could be one with a storm at night I couldn't fathom but that was what I saw. I tried to envision a picture that would bring out that essence and failed because I couldn't wrap my artist's imagination around what I was seeing.

We sat in comfortable silence until we found ourselves nodding off and, with embarrassed expressions, we both at the same time said that it was time for bed. I pointed him towards the loft with a double bed that my parents used and, as he climbed that ladder, I climbed the second one to the loft with the teddy bear rug.

In bed, warm and comfortable, I couldn't sleep. Instead, I listened to the storm beyond the walls and wondered what it would be like to be stranded in that white, isolated world with no safe place nearby, no food, and little hope of rescue. It could have happened to him. Not to us both now, of course, because we were safe in a sturdy log cabin, but the thought made me shudder until I put the pillow over my head and slept.

CHAPTER 4

In the morning, the first thing we did after descending from our lofts was go to the window to see what the world was like in the light of day, hoping against hope that we'd been wrong and the snow we'd seen had been just a winter's kiss instead of the beginning of a full-blown blizzard.

No such luck.

The outside world was beautiful in its own way and I thought in some remote part of my mind that it would make a lovely picture, with black and brown tree trunks and green pine needles, all enveloped in snow that varied from blue where it lay in shadows to pristine, virginal white in more open spots, and a few multi-colored drifts where it had been swirled into various odd shapes. Like the one that was my car only now it was covered by who knew how much snow and was an indistinct, unrecognizable lump.

More important, though, was that we saw everything through a veil of still more snow falling steadily, thickly and persistently from the sky beyond the treetops. Looking up, the sky was invisible. All we saw were billions of snowflakes cartwheeling down. There was wind up there, too. We could feel it though the thick trees kept it at bay nearer the ground.

"I was hoping I was wrong," was all my visitor said, with a huge sigh.

"Unfortunately, you were right. That's a real, old-fashioned blizzard out there."

We stared out the window until it occurred to me that we'd been together overnight and didn't even know one another's name. Dumb. I turned to him and said, "I'm Laurie." No last names, we wouldn't be together long enough to need them. Would we?'

He held out a hand and I took it and we solemnly shook hands as a grin started at one corner of his mouth and spread across it and then jumped through the air and landed on me and we found ourselves laughing like a couple of idiots because we were both thinking the same thing. How had we managed to ignore the fundamental courtesy of exchanging names?

"I'm Jase, and I own the event center. It's a fair distance from here, which is why I didn't start walking home when my snowmobile died." He rubbed the back of his neck. "I figured the road would be closer and I'd flag someone down. Good thing I didn't, no one would be on the road in weather like this. And a very good thing that I saw your tracks." Then, with a grimace, "Sorry, of course you don't know what I'm talking about. I'm so wrapped up in my somewhat new acquisition that I assume everyone knows about the event center even though that's a blatant, arrogant assumption on my part."

"Not at all, I've heard about it. Everyone has." I withdrew my hand with a slight flush because neither of us seemed to realize we'd been shaking hands way longer than usual. "I've heard lots of good things. Like that it's an awesome place."

"That's a relief." We stared at one another and tried to come up with something else to say until we realized that morning is breakfast time so I opened the cupboards to see what was available. "We can finish the eggs. Then I won't have to carry them home. And there's a fair-sized slab of bacon."

I reached for the bacon and was stopped by Jase's hand on my arm. "Let's not eat that yet." He examined the contents of the refrigerator while pretending not to, a subtle alarm spreading over his face at how little was in it. "Just in case we're here for a while what say we stretch the supplies until we know how long it'll be?"

He smiled to take the sting from his words and shrugged as if it was no big deal that the food inside was limited while not fooling me for a minute. Concern nibbled the edges of that subtle expression, turning it into full-blown concern as neither of us could avoid the fact that there wasn't an unlimited supply of food.

He shrugged and tried to act casual. "It'll be easier for you to throw any extras in the car when we leave than to go hungry because we ate it all too soon." And then, giving up on pretending things were normal, he caved and his face sobered. "I'm so sorry. My presence here makes things worse. There are two of us. If I'd not come, you'd have plenty."

I pulled out the eggs and left the bacon in the refrigerator. "I'd never get over it if I learned someone suffered in the blizzard near the cabin while I was comfortable in here." I shuddered and had a hard time stopping until I forced my body to be still because I didn't want him to know how shook I was by his comment about supplies and about what it was like outside. Mostly about how little food we had.

We made breakfast. We worked well together and ended up with a decent meal that we ate seated on opposite sides of the scarred and wobbly wood table that had been in the cabin since forever. Then we cleaned the kitchen together and looked around and realized that there was an entire day ahead of us, and that meant hours of doing something. But what?

"Do you like to read?" I pointed to the shelves that consisted of our fairly extensive library because, with no TV or cell service, reading is a great option. He nodded and examined them for a moment before pulling out one of my father's favorites. Jaws.

I smiled privately as he dropped into the chair beside the stove and began reading the story all men seem to like, and soon he forgot I existed, which was fine with me because it meant I didn't have to play hostess. My lack of social graces wasn't important if he was reading.

Which left me to think what I'd do with the day that stretched ahead. My fingers itched to sketch something. Anything. Outside would be best, with black trees with snow piled thick on the branches and perhaps that bright, red Cardinal. But it was warm in the cabin and that warmth held me in thrall, not to mention that it might be bad manners to desert my uninvited guest, at least until he was oriented to the place.

But the itch grew, so I looked around for something inside to paint but I'd already memorialized the room a thousand times over the years. Besides, the restlessness brought on by the storm made me want something different. Something new. But what?

My gaze moved until it rested on the sandy head of the man now lost in the story of a dangerous shark. I was caught by the flicker of firelight on his cheekbones. The half-smile as he followed the adventures of the intrepid sheriff. The way one leg was slung over the arm of the chair and moved back and forth ever so slightly as he grew more and more involved in the story.

I'd paint my visitor. I'd never gone in for portraits but this wasn't for sale, it was for passing the time and, in a moment of internal honesty, I admitted that it was also for me to see if I could pull it off. If I could do a portrait. If I could capture that quality in him that went so well with his surroundings. That made him look so right seated beside the wood stove.

I thought once again how well he blended into the cabin and its furnishings. He had the same tone on tone brown skin as the cabin's log walls had from years of the same kind of weathering that he'd got from being outside. He appeared just as sturdily made as the cabin and sat with a laid back, relaxed manner that all families want when on vacation. He was a man of the forest and of this place and time.

The errant thought struck me that his event center must do well if guests got the same vibe from him that I did, and I wondered if they felt it as strongly or was it just the artist in me that excited my senses as I headed for my pencils?

I quietly opened the case I'd so carefully shut the night before, pulled out a pencil, and set to work, pleased and somewhat surprised at how well and how quickly it went until I glanced at the clock and discovered that more time had passed than I'd realized.

Noon was near, the portrait was coming together nicely, the snow beyond the window continued to fall, and the wind above the treetops continued to blow. I put my pencil down.

Jase looked up, eyes gleaming. "Can I move now?"

I flushed. "I didn't realize you knew I was drawing you."

"Kind of obvious. Can I see?" I showed him. His eyes went wide. "Are you an artist or something?" I nodded. "A real artist?"

I laughed. "My pictures are in a gallery and people do buy them. Does that count?"

"Absolutely." He looked me up and down. "I know several amateur artists and some of them are quite good, but you're my first professional." The eyes gleamed again. "You don't look like an artist. No strange, billowy clothes and dangly earrings."

"Sorry, I never learned how to be artsy." I raked my hand through my hair. My short, practical, red hair. "A failure my agent bemoans frequently."

He examined me again, slower this time. "His problem. Normal is nice even if your hair is red."

"Red hair is normal."

"Normal for some families, I suppose but it could be considered artsy if you let it grow long enough and put some sparkly stuff in it." He examined the almost finished sketch again. "Can I have it?"

"When it's done. This is just a beginning, a sketch. The finished portrait will take a while but I promise to give it to you." Which was when I realized I had a specific picture in mind. Cabin, man, and atmosphere, with trees and snow seen through the window. A different kind of forest picture, but I had a gut feeling that it would be good.

We had bacon for lunch, along with toast that almost finished the bread but I'd given up on a trek through the forest to see if the Cardinal was back and, after the concern about supplies, I decided that we needed the bread more than the birds did. We cleaned up quietly, both thinking of the food in the refrigerator and cupboard – the almost empty refrigerator and cupboard -- while wondering how long the storm would last.

And how long we'd have to wait after it ended before we'd be rescued. No thought of driving any more, the snow was already too deep for my car. And there was no way to call for help, something he didn't know but should be told. I took a deep breath. "There's no cell service here." My words came from nowhere. I couldn't stop them.

A long pause. Then, "Does anyone know you're here?" His gaze flicked to the window and beyond, to where the useless car was buried beneath a mound of white.

"My parents left a couple days ago. They knew I stayed on, but I told them I'd probably leave Sunday."

"They'll figure things out when you don't get home."

"I have my own apartment." I faced him and looked straight into his eyes. "We communicate often but sometimes time gets away from us all and we go weeks without calling."

His breath was deep and slow, a deliberate thing on his part so he'd appear normal but his eyes were wide and kept expressionless with effort. "I live alone, too. No one knows where I am and I can't think of anyone with a reason to check."

He went to the window and stared into the white world. "What about the road? How long after the storm ends until it's plowed?"

I waited until he turned back before answering. "The cabin is usually empty in the winter and we're the last place on a road that's barely used. This visit was a fluke, an impromptu vacation because the snow wasn't deep so we knew the road would be drivable. It usually isn't in the winter."

"So no snowplow until spring?"

"That's right."

His held breath finally came out long and slow as he fought to keep concern from what I'd already figured was a normally sunny expression. His effort failed completely.

CHAPTER 5

The cozy atmosphere of the morning evaporated. Jase found another book but I suspected he had no idea what he was reading and his body language was now all wrong for the portrait unless I wanted to turn it into something tense and uncomfortable and I didn't. I wanted to capture the subtle, warm essence that had filled the cabin before we looked out the window. So I shoved the half-finished sketch aside and looked around.

I had to do something or go crazy thinking about supplies and time and whether or not we'd be rescued but even with all that on my mind, or perhaps because of all that, my fingers still itched to sketch the forest in the winter. I had few pictures of winter because the weather seldom cooperated enough for me to come north at that time of year.

I decided that I would not just sit and worry. Would not! I went to the window and looked outside and mentally measured the snow to see if it was too deep for me to get through. The Cardinal wouldn't be held back by snow on the forest floor, it could fly freely because the trees broke the wind and its only concern would be flakes falling, and that red bird flying through white flakes would be gorgeous if only I could find it again.

As I considered the outside world, I realized that that snow wasn't coming down quite as thickly as earlier. A temporary break in the blizzard? Perhaps. It happens, sometimes.

So I quietly gathered my sketch pad and pencils and dressed in all the warm things I'd brought with me and slipped outside so silently that Jase, who now must be involved in the story of a rogue shark even though he couldn't have been earlier in spite of what it looked like because he knew I was sketching him, didn't look up as I left.

The snow was light and blew up in puffs as I walked, which was good because it was a lot deeper than when I'd made the same trek a day earlier. I knew the forest intimately and wouldn't get lost, not even with everything changed and different beneath a fluffy dress of white.

That dress was trimmed in more white and still more white stuff hung dangerously low from branches and twigs, waiting for a stiff breeze to send it exploding onto the frozen world. I wished I could stay and watch and possibly get that explosion on paper but I was on a mission to find the Cardinal of the day before. No more boredom for me.

It wasn't especially cold and I soon found myself overheating, so I opened my parka and stuffed my mittens in pockets as I headed for the spot where I'd last seen the bright, red bird. And there he was, with his more soberly colored wife beside him, both perched on a branch not too high above me.

I hardly dared breathe and pulled my sketch pad

out slowly so as not to spook them. Then just as slowly I dropped into the snow and folded my legs, the sound thankfully muffled by its insulating quality, and then I riffled through the book to the last page, the one that had been waiting for this special picture though, when I'd left it blank I hadn't known what would eventually fill it. Just that something would because something always did. The forest never disappointed me and the Cardinal that had appeared so unexpectedly the previous day was perfect.

I bent my head and began sketching, wondering what would happen if I deliberately made a sound and sent the Cardinal pair into the air. Would I see how they flew and get their movements on paper? Or would they simply fly away and leave me with nothing?

As I wondered I heard a slight sound, muffled by the snow but definitely coming my way. Uneasily I wished I'd brought something to use as a weapon though I couldn't imagine what that would be. A broom, maybe? The poker I used to stir the fire? But I had nothing and turned slowly and quietly towards the direction of the soft sound to confront whatever was headed towards me.

And saw Jase, aware that I was sketching the Cardinals and moving as quietly as possible so as not to disturb them, but definitely joining me. The thick fur around the hood of his parka made it impossible to see his face so I had no idea why he was there. Was the cabin on fire? Did he want to know what was for dinner? Or something else?

When he came beside me, he simply sank downward into the snow until we were at eye level and then he peered at the sketch I was working on. He flipped his hood back to show keen interest in my work and I saw a spark that showed the primal need of human beings for companionship. He'd come into the forest simply because that was where another person – me --could be found and he wanted to be there too.

He stretched out those long legs slowly, inch by inch, so as not to send the Cardinals flying away and indicated by a slight nod of his head and the gleam in his eyes that I was to continue and that he'd like to watch if it was okay with me.

Was it? Of course it was, so I turned back to my half-finished sketch and we sat that way for the better part of an hour, Jase watching and me sketching and the Cardinals on their tree branch doing whatever Cardinals do. Until they suddenly, unexpectedly, both at the same moment though I'd have sworn there'd been no communication between them, rose into the air and after circling beneath the tree branches a couple times they were gone.

"Beautiful." The first words Jase said out loud, looking at the sketch and seemingly also at me and, more slowly, the surrounding forest. "Absolutely beautiful."

I felt that look clear through me, all the way to my toes, and there was no reason to feel it so powerfully but I did and I knew as surely as the sun comes up in the morning that I'd do no more sketching that day because, somehow, with Jase's arrival wearing a smile that could have melted the snow, that the artist in me was suddenly on vacation, replaced by a more sociable person, one that seldom came to the fore of my consciousness because I'm pretty much a loner. But I didn't want to be one now. Because of that smile.

I smiled back and his smile grew broader and then dimmed somewhat. "I hope I didn't scare them off."

"I'm sure you didn't. Where'd you learn to move so quietly?"

"It comes in handy when I take guests at the Center for nature walks. If I scare all the wildlife away, they won't see anything and then they won't come back." He considered the almost finished sketch. "Will this go on someone's wall?"

"This is a sketch, like the one of you in the cabin. The finished picture will be much larger and in color and I hope someone buys it."

He pointed to the black and white pencil lines. "I'm glad because Cardinals are normally red." He thought over his words. "Except for the females, of course, but they are lovely too in their own way."

Again, I felt that odd sensation shoot through me and wondered why I was reacting so strongly to such a mundane statement. I told myself I'd better get a grip on myself because we'd be spending some time together and it wouldn't do to go into a tailspin whenever he said something. Anything. Or smiled as he was smiling now.

What on earth was wrong with me? I decided that I'd been alone for way too long. Way, way too long! In the future, I'd be smart to be more social. But as I considered my reaction to Jase I told myself that he was somewhat of an unusual person. Charismatic.

I looked towards where the sky was hiding behind the gray of the day and the white of the falling snow. "I don't know exactly what time it is but I suspect we'd better get back to the cabin before the storm decides to kick in again and what feeble light there is disappears."

I tipped my head a bit and studied the forest. "These are the short days of the year, you know. Dusk comes in the middle of the afternoon."

He nodded and rose in one smooth motion, then held out a hand and pulled me up beside him. I was stiff from sitting cross legged for so long and would have toppled over if not for his grip on my hand and he grinned at my fumbling and had to stop himself from laughing.

I dropped his hand quickly as stability returned and then I cocked my head as I examined him head to toe and tipped my nose up a bit but wasn't able to hold my imperious pose and, unbidden, I let out the laughter that was bubbling up from somewhere in me that had been triggered by what I'd already figured was charisma and that unfailingly wonderful smile.

When he saw me laughing he stopped trying to control himself and laughed too, a deep, pleasant baritone that would have echoed through the forest in the summer but was muffled by the snow that fell gently all around us, enclosing us in a world that was small and private both as to sight and sound.

Then he took my sketchbook and turned on his heel to head back to the cabin, saying something about carrying it because he didn't want to chance me falling and losing all those beautiful pictures and I heard the choked sound of laughter as he went fast enough to dodge any snowballs I might send in his direction. And I was suddenly very glad that this stranger had gone snowmobiling and ended up in my family's cabin in a blizzard. Because he was – nice. And now I didn't have to experience a blizzard in the forest all alone and that was an odd thought for a would-be hermit like me.

CHAPTER 6

That fizzy sensation in my innards continued after we were safely and warmly in the cabin and hanging up our outer wear, all of it, which took a while. Then we simply continued on, as comfortable with each other as if we'd been living together forever, odd as that sounds.

Was it because I almost fell and we laughed about it? Or were we comfortable with each other because we were stranded in a blizzard without hope of rescue so we'd have to depend on each other and difficult situations always go best when people get along? I didn't know why I felt so comfortable with him and, after a moment of reflection, decided that the 'why' didn't matter. It was enough to enjoy the inner tingle that added to the heat of the wood stove and the gas one we cooked dinner on.

We were very careful not to overdo in the food department and didn't mention the alarming way our supplies were disappearing because what good would it do? We smiled instead at each tiny clumsiness that happened as we prepared a simple meal that we ate at the wobbly wood table that made the soup slosh each time we took another spoonful. Soup that we made without any discussion as to what the menu would be because we both knew that food goes farther in soup than any other dish.

Then it was evening. The time passed quickly and so did the night that followed that consisted of dark, windswept hours spent listening to the blizzard on the other side of the log walls. Morning was at first just a slightly lighter version of that dark because the sun, high and safe above the storm, might as well not have existed.

I was almost grateful for the whiteness of the snow because as the morning progressed and that unseen but brilliant sun high above the storm reached what must have been its zenith, the world turned lighter, almost as if there'd been nothing blocking those rays because the white snow make everything appear as if through a snow prism.

By then, of course, it being high noon, we were once more involved in ways to pass the time, Jase reading another novel and me putting finishing touches on the sketch of him beside the wood stove because today, as when I'd started my sketch, he was humming contentedly while moving one foot slightly up and down as he lost himself, this time in Treasure Island.

My parents had long ago made sure the cabin library was stocked with classical works because they were canny people who knew the value of decent reading material lying casually around when boredom set in. I consider myself something of an expert on the classics.

He sighed when he reached the end, shut Treasure Island, and returned it to the shelf laden with books. He then perused the rest but shook his head ever so slightly in a way that said he'd read enough for now and then continued on to other shelves that contained the board games that we played during the long evenings when no one was ready to sleep and the mosquitoes outside were too vicious to allow anyone outside who was averse to being eaten alive.

"Do you play Monopoly?" He reached for the game but hesitated as he waited for an answer.

"I'm not a champion, that's reserved for my dad, but I can give it a half-hearted try."

His shoulders shook with more of the silent laughter that I was learning was a part of him and then he turned towards me, grinning widely. I liked that grin and decided that it was one of the better parts of his nice-guy persona and I was glad I was stranded with a decent person.

"That's good. I was afraid you were going to say you're the world's best player and then I'd have to pass because you'd whip me soundly." He pulled the game out and headed for the table. "As it is, it sounds as if we're at about the same level. So what about it? Want to play?"

By the time the outside world was completely dark once more, we'd learned that, as he'd surmised, we were about equal in the game playing department. Neither good enough to brag about our prowess but good enough to at least get through without too many gaffes.

As he put away the Monopoly board, we both found ourselves glancing outside. Jase frowned. "It doesn't seem to be letting up."

"It's been – what? – two days now?"

"Few blizzards last longer than two days. Three at

the most."

"Tomorrow should be the end, then. If it snows at all tomorrow it'll most likely be less intense. Less snow coming down. Not as dark." Not as scary, though I didn't say that out loud.

"We'll be able to take stock and see what we have to contend with in order to get out of here." He frowned again and finally, quietly, said what I was sure he hoped would make me feel better. "And we will get out of here. We'll do something. Figure some way." And, yes, it did settle some of that queasiness that had found its way to my stomach.

"Of course we will." The words were pure bravado on my part. "We'll be fine." But my glance swerved away from the window because I didn't want to see snow any longer. I'd seen enough. It just kept falling and falling and piling up everywhere and setting my teeth on edge.

I'd look again only when it was done falling and when I saw the pristine white level in some places and piled in others and all of it clean but most of all, not falling from the sky. No more coming down. None. Then and only then, I'd smile.

We had more of the soup for dinner and I found some stale crackers I hadn't known existed and we pretended we'd had a great meal. Which we had in a way, finishing up the left-overs of the left-overs had made an unexpectedly good soup. But with each bowl, we knew we were getting closer to the end of the food supply.

Which would happen all too soon and when we reached the absolute end, then what?

One thing we had in abundance was coffee,

probably enough to keep an army or two marching non-stop for a week. So that night, long after midnight, when the wind beyond the log walls was still blowing as hard as ever and I couldn't sleep no matter how I tried because I was listening for it to start slowing down and thinking with a sinking heart that it might not, ever, I climbed down from my loft, found the coffee pot, and made myself a full pot.

When it was ready, I poured a cup and slid down to a comfortable spot on the fuzzy rug on the floor before the wood stove, shoved another stick of wood on top of the ones that were slowly dying and watched as it caught, flared, and settled down to a steady burn. Then I leaned against the couch to enjoy a drink.

"Mind if I join you?" Jase peered at me from his greater height, hands on knees as he bent closer and spoke. "Nothing can match the aroma of fresh coffee as far as I'm concerned and it's pretty strong and woke me up and drew me right here."

"Sorry. I didn't mean to wake you."

"I love coffee."

I pointed to the coffee pot and indicated the space beside me and soon he was there, sighing in contentment as he took his first sip and leaned back against the couch and crossed those long legs of his beside mine. "Pure heaven and very good coffee. Someone knows how to choose the perfect blend"

I swirled my coffee and stared into it as if doing so would give me some special insights as to our plight. Then I sighed mightily and said what we'd carefully not said up to that point. "We have to talk."

He perused his coffee as if the black depths held answers. "I know. We've been avoiding it but, in a way, it doesn't do any good to make plans until the blizzard ends and we know what we have to contend with."

"I suppose that's right." I didn't want to discuss the future any more than he did and so, somehow, we went back to leaning against the couch and toasting our toes at the stove as we drank cup after cup of coffee. My parents like coffee and they only stock the best everywhere they have the ability to do so. The cabin was no exception.

I giggled and said the first thing either of us had said about our shrinking food supply. "We might run out of food but we'll be able to drink like royalty."

He raised his cup like a toast. "It's strong stuff. If we drink enough, maybe we'll be able to up and fly away on caffeine alone."

And then it happened. A lessening of the wind howling high above the trees. In our minds we could see the tops of the evergreens bending a little less. We held our breaths and looked at each other. "Is it over?"

"Maybe." That one word, of hope and possibility kept us awake and reasonably happy until the coffee was gone and we were so tired that even caffeine couldn't keep us awake and we climbed to our respective lofts and slept.

CHAPTER 7

Morning came bright and clear, with only a thin veil of snow still falling. I was disappointed to see it but soon realized that as it swirled and moved voids appeared between the sheets of white stuff with numerous bright layers dancing over and under one another. Movement meant there was still wind somewhere above but the veil itself was fading, disappearing slowly, almost gone, and the brightness meant the sun was slicing through those layers now and then.

"The blizzard is history!" I didn't know I was shouting until Jase peered over the ledge of his loft to see what the commotion was about, and then he shinnied down the ladder so fast I doubted his feet hit the steps and he joined me at the window where I'd pulled the curtain all the way back the better to see the developing peaceful world beyond.

I heard his indrawn breath as he contemplated our small world, bound by evergreens and snowdrifts. That sigh didn't sound as happy as I felt and he said slowly, "There's a lot of snow out there."

"Yes there is, but it's done. The blizzard is done." Didn't he understand?

"It's not waist deep, thank goodness, but it's deep enough."

"We should celebrate." How could he not be dancing with happiness?

"We should look for wood."

His simple words forced me to return to the nasty reality of our situation and contemplate our pathetically small pile of wood as he asked, "Do you know if there are sticks on the ground? Think we can find any beneath all that snow?" His forehead was wrinkled with concern.

I peered soberly at the wood pile, forgetting my earlier shouts of happiness. "What we have won't last long, will it?"

"What's out there that we can get easily?"

I thought about the area around the cabin, whether there were branches on the ground. "A few sticks might be in the yard."

"Under all that snow."

My shoulders sank. "A lot of snow and not many sticks if I remember right."

"Not enough to be worth digging for." He looked around a second time. "There are dead branches on the trees above the snow but low enough to reach. We can break those off and burn them."

His gaze was on the evergreens surrounding the cabin. As the forest grew the trees reached ever upwards and sent all nutrients to the top, causing the lower branches to die off. Those dead, dry branches were close enough to the ground for us to grab and break them off. As I followed his gaze, I realized that we could collect a fair number of small branches.

But how long would they last? I screwed up my

courage and asked the question we were both thinking. "How much wood will we need?"

His frown matched mine. "If the temperature drops, as it most likely will, more than what's out there because no one knows we're here and who knows how long before they figure it out and come for us."

We stared silently at the trees, wishing there were more branches. Wishing we could get the ones on the ground, too. But the snow was too deep, and the standing dead branches were limited. I licked my lips, then realized what doing so looked like and stopped.

I turned from the window, examined the interior of the cabin, found my gaze settling on the pantry and forgot about wood as I thought how limited our food supply was and that made me sick with worry so I looked away again and, unable to consider either wood or food, chose to look at Jase because he was the only positive thing in my life at the moment, only to find him looking at me with the same expression I knew was on my face.

We were both scared. Terrified.

He blinked. Looked away, then back. Cleared his throat and said slowly and without a glimmer of the smile I'd learned was a part of him, "We have decisions to make because if we can't expect help, we must save ourselves."

He turned back to the window and stared long and silently at the green and black and white world beyond. "I'll amend that statement. We *know* we won't get help which means we *must* decide what to do and we won't last long here. So the way I see it, the only important decision to be made is where to go and when to leave."

He turned to the kitchen area and rubbed his belly

while once again putting on that smile that had been missing moments earlier and it's appearance amazed me until, as I kept watching, I realized it was real, though I couldn't figure out how he could feel good in such dire circumstances until he said, "Which we will discuss after breakfast because I'm hungry and I don't think well on an empty stomach."

His statement was so unexpected that I exploded in laughter. How'd he manage to make me laugh? Was it a deliberate attempt to lighten a dangerous situation or was it simply Jase being himself?

Then I realized that the man was hungry and at the moment perhaps that was more important than figuring out what to do. Maybe. And perhaps it was the right thing to think about because we couldn't do anything about our situation at the moment so we might as well have breakfast.

Still, the situation was so ridiculous and the change from terror to hunger so unexpected that I found myself grinning along with him and, just like that, the mood in the cabin that had started out as a celebration of the end of the blizzard when I first rose and then turned into despair as we faced our future had somehow changed again, this time to comfortable, and I wondered if ever before had I experienced so many wildly different moods in such a short span of time.

As we ate oatmeal that I'd found stuck in the back corner of the cupboard that was so old I didn't even look at the 'sell-by' date, Jase leaned back thoughtfully as he carefully and slowly savored each and every bite and said, "There's everything we need and more at the Center." His eyes narrowed and he moved forward again and leaned across the table until we were nose to nose. "If we can get there."

"How far is it, exactly?" My question followed a long, measured silence as we both contemplated the changed world and whether we could get through the deeper snow. Before the blizzard, there'd been a thin cover of it. Now there were inches. In some places, many inches.

"I'm not sure. I came by way of the snowmobile trail and that winds around a lot. Do you have a map of the area?"

"Actually, yes. We have a topographic map." I flushed. "My dad got it a while back. He loves to peruse it and think about going places without actually getting out of his chair." I indicated the chair beside the wood stove that Jase had occupied while reading books. "While he looks it over, he's seated in a comfortable chair and going someplace would require getting up and leaving his warm, comfy situation so it never happens but he enjoys thinking about it."

"He comes here to relax, and it sounds like that's what he does." A smile ghosted across his face. "I think I'd like your dad."

I found the large book with topographic maps of the entire area, spread it across the table, and opened it to the page where the cabin was located. I pointed. "Here's where we are."

He pored over the map for a minute, then put a finger on another spot. "That's where the snowmobile died. I came here with little effort in the middle of the night so I'm fairly sure we can get that far at least without much trouble." The finger moved and stopped farther away. "Here's the Center."

Not so far on the map. Mere inches. Miles of forest

and fields in the real world. His face darkened as he figured the distance. "How far is it? Can you tell?" He peered at the map and tried to convert inches into miles. "Think we can make it?" His question echoed in the cabin.

I took the map from him and turned it to see better. I know the forest. I've spent hours, days, weeks and months wandering about until what was lines and elevations on the map was as real to me as if I was looking at the ground itself. "We'll never make it if we go the way you came on your snowmobile." I shook my head. "Too many twists and turns, which is good for snowmobile trails and bad for walking."

"Is there another way?" His voice had a tinge of something I didn't want to think about. Despair. "The road won't be usable until it's plowed, and we don't know when that'll happen so we can't walk out to it and wait for a passerby."

"It's never used in the winter so it won't be plowed until spring." I examined the map again, calculating miles. "The Center may be an option." I traced a path through the forest and hope rose in my chest. "I know a short cut."

He nibbled his lower lip and peered closer at the map, following my finger. "Through a bog." He breathed in deeply. "I know the bog. The Center is on the edge. It's large and it's nasty."

"It'll be frozen solid this time of year."

"But there are no trees. It's all open." The blizzard could have laid down feet upon feet of snow there. "What about drifts? What about wind?"

We stared at one another as he asked slowly, "If we try it and make it to the bog and we're exhausted from tromping through the snow and find that we can't get across the bog, can we come back?"

I took a deep breath. "I don't know."

"How long will it take to reach the Center if everything goes right? Best guess."

"A day." I decided to be honest. "A long day."

"One day. Just one day. But that's a lot of hours in the cold and snow." We stared at one another until he said it for both of us, his voice harsh and grating. "It's our only choice. Our only chance to reach safety. To survive."

We were silent so long that the lack of sound screamed until Jase snapped the book of maps shut and said, "Right now, let's get some of those dead branches for firewood and in the process find out what that snow is like. Maybe it's light and fluffy. Easy walking. Maybe it's hard and crusted and there's no chance of going anywhere." So we pulled on every warm thing we owned and went outside.

He was right about the snow. It was light and flew every which way, making white clouds each time we took a step. We found ourselves grinning even as we snapped off tree branch after tree branch and carried them through that white fluff back to the cabin where we deposited them on the porch. Later we'd take them inside but there was no reason to open the door and let the cold inside any more than necessary.

Soon, somehow, against all reason or perhaps because Jase was Jase and smiles were a part of his being, in that white, fluffy world we found ourselves laughing and as we dropped the last load of branches on the porch we realized that we were standing in a winter wonderland. Without consulting each other, without even looking into each other's face for permission, and again against all reason but perhaps because it was a part of Jase's personality, we started to play.

"Snow angels?" Soon Jase was on his back on the ground trying to make snow angels and failing miserably because the snow was too deep and fluffy for him to make any headway. But he tried until he ended up with snow on his face and every other part of him and then he had to stand up and shake himself like a dog to change from a snowman back into himself.

"We have a sled in the shed." I pointed to the small shed not far from the cabin where we kept the few things necessary to keep the place operational. An axe, the sled, clippers to cut dangerous, low-hanging branches. That sort of thing. "And there's a hill not far from here."

He shook his head, still wiggling from his snow angel fiasco. "Too much light snow. It'll plow through it instead of sliding over it and we'll get lost in a blizzard of our own making."

"It's a plastic sled. It'll work better than one with runners." I loved that sled. My uncle brought it north to haul deer during hunting season but he was a lousy hunter. I don't think it was ever used and it still hung in pristine newness on the wall of the ancient shed, high up and out of the way. "Want to go sledding?"

He sighed and put a hand to the small of his back. "Maybe later. Right now I could use a cup of strong, hot coffee and a chair beside that warm fire."

I nodded agreement. "Maybe for the best." We'd need a ladder to reach the sled and the only ladder on the property was so rickety that my father had admonished me sternly against using it. "Emergency vehicles would have a hard time getting down that ridiculous driveway if anyone broke a leg." But I said nothing to Jase because we'd decided not to go sledding.

CHAPTER 8

We carried the wood on the porch inside by the arms full. With just that short time with the door open and a lot of cold wood brought inside, the inside temperature dropped enough that we put several additional sticks on the fire and watched with appreciation as they caught and roared red and orange and very, very hot. And then Jase commandeered that chair beside the stove and lolled in pure luxury.

He raised his head enough to see out the window. "I wish this blizzard had waited until it was supposed to start." He gazed at me with a look that was part enjoyment, part fear for what lay ahead, and part something I couldn't read. "But I still love the forest, and in winter it's special and I'm glad I'm here and glad we met."

"Me too." I dropped to the floor beside his chair and in front of the stove and put my hands out to gather in the warmth. "I've always loved the forest, summer and winter. Always will." I followed his look outside. "Yes, it's cold out and dangerous but we have a plan."

I tipped my chin up because the forest was my friend and I refused to be afraid even if a coldness was gathering in the pit of my stomach. "We'll be okay.

We'll make it. We may have been blindsided by a blizzard that came too early but the world isn't ending and we are both healthy and in good shape."

"We can walk." He grinned and lightly touched my hair and watched as it flew every which way, which it does. He smiled and I had the odd thought that he was comparing my red hair to the fire. "We will take a winter's walk to the Center, that's what we'll do." Then he added, "I love taking walks."

He slumped deeper into the chair and put his own hands towards the stove as his expression changed somewhat into something I didn't recognize. Didn't want to know what it meant because there was a darkness to it and I didn't want to think what caused it. "We should go soon, though, before the snow has a chance to pack enough to be hard walking. We don't want to wait until there's a crust we'll have to break through."

I nodded thoughtfully, glad that this man knew about the forest. Neither of us were experts but between us we knew enough to survive. I hoped.

As I stared into the fire, I realized that the brief time playing in the snow had done something to my insides. Strengthened me. Primed me for what lay ahead. Made me realize that it was snow. Just snow.

I could handle a walk to the Center through the deep, white, snow and temperatures that would plummet because they always do after a blizzard. I could do it.

"Yes." The simple agreement didn't seem enough so I said more. "You're right, though. We should leave soon, before the temperature really drops."

I withdrew my hands from the warmth and

examined them rather than Jase as he indicated the window, with lacy frost spreading across the pane. "Too late for that, I think. I'll bet that if we go outside, it'll be colder than when we gathered firewood."

"Already?" Sometimes the cold waited a day or so before descending in the aftermath of a blizzard.

"I'm afraid the cold has arrived."

Not that it mattered, we had no choice. But there was a bit of leeway as to when we took that walk. I looked at the wind-up clock. "Too late to leave today. It'll be dark soon."

"Tomorrow, then, at first light. We should get ready now. Make packs to carry food and water and extra clothes and blankets in case we need them."

I nodded. "I'll look through the closets and see what I can find."

By the time it was dark enough to turn on the kerosene lamp and stop long enough to put together most of the last of the leftovers and call it a meal, we had our packs ready. Jase gave me a suddenly sober look. "Get a good night's sleep. We need all the rest we can get."

I set the alarm for four-thirty the next morning, knowing it would still be full dark for several hours but thinking I knew the immediate area well enough to get us off to a good start so by daylight we'd be well on our way.

We climbed to our respective lofts and I rolled into blankets that would be added to the packs in the morning. And then, expecting that I'd not sleep a wink, I fell so deeply asleep that I didn't wake until the alarm went off.

Once up, I threw the covers over the railing and

slid down the ladder, after which I added them to my pack. Then I looked towards Jase's loft to see if he was ready. I neither saw nor heard anything, so I climbed back to my loft and looked across the space between but it was too dark to see anything. But nothing moved, so he must still be sleeping.

He should get up. We should get going. I slid down my ladder a second time and climbed up his as noisily as possible so if he wasn't quite awake that would do the job. At the top, I peered into the loft my parents used when they were at the cabin. And saw an empty bed, blankets removed. I looked down and saw Jase's pack with the blankets tied securely to it.

So where was he? I climbed down slowly, thinking, and, as I stared at the two considerable packs, I knew where he'd gone. To the shed. To get the sled. The one that could tow everything and save us the extra weight. The one that could be reached only by climbing a ladder that could fall apart any moment.

I felt a cold settle in my middle at the thought of that rickety ladder and said a brief prayer that the ladder had held but my stomach kept plummeting downwards.

I climbed quickly into my outerwear and followed his tracks to the shed. And found him on the floor with the sled beside him and the ladder – now broken completely – a few feet away. He was staring at one leg, not moving. He was swearing quietly but steadily.

He heard me and looked up, anguish in his expression. "The ladder broke. I fell." He felt his leg carefully and winced. "I did something to my leg." He shook his head in total frustration and anger. "I'm so sorry. I don't think I can walk." And, with an indrawn breath, "I ruined everything."

I dropped to his side and felt the leg he was holding. "I had a class in first aid." His snow pants were thick but I could feel the bones of his leg through them. "I didn't learn much but I'm fairly sure that it's not broken and that's something. That's good."

"It's not good if I can't walk. And I can't." His tone had a finality to it that couldn't be argued with. "I tried but, as you can see, I'm still on the floor."

"Let's get you inside." I grabbed the sled and put it alongside him. "Then we'll see what's what and figure out what to do."

"I'm so sorry." He repeated the phrase several times as I rolled him onto the sled and pulled it to the porch, after which, with both of us doing our best, I helped him upright, then up the stairs and across the porch, and then inside where I carefully removed his outer clothing and examined the leg in more detail. The whole operation, from looking for him when I realized he wasn't in his loft to bringing him inside took more than an hour. No more early start for us.

"Not broken," I repeated. "That's good but your whole leg is swollen."

"I twisted as I fell. Who knows what I tore, ripped, strained, sprained or whatever?" He looked at his leg as if he wished it would disappear. "You go without me. Get to the Center. When you get there, call for help." He swallowed. "I'll be fine."

I looked around the cabin. "No you won't so that's not an option. No food, not enough wood and how would you get it and put it into the stove if there was more?" I swallowed hard as the only way out of our situation started growing in my mind.

"Besides, how would emergency people get here?

They'd have to plow the road and then the driveway and who knows how long that would take?" I shook my head. "You're not staying here. You can't."

"I can't walk." He pointed to his leg.

"We have a sled. I'll pull you. And the provisions."

"All the way to the Center?" He shook his head. "Not possible."

I took a deep breath because I knew what I was saying and how difficult it would be, but I also knew with a certainty that couldn't be challenged that my plan was the only option available. "I can do it." And I made myself stare at him and forced a calm, unconcerned expression onto my face so he'd believe me though inside I was trembling.

Could I do it? I wasn't sure. I only knew that I had to try and that, with God's help because He was the only one who knew where we were and what was happening, we'd make it to the Center. If not? I refused to think about it.

Jase said nothing, just stared at me until he accepted that I was going to do this no matter how much he argued. Until he simply said, "When do we start?"

I checked the time. Hours had passed, the sun was bright on the snow. "Not today. Today we rest and get your leg wrapped as securely as I can manage so it'll be stable during the trip. You won't be able to bend it. That'll be good. We leave early in the morning. Four at the latest. Maybe before then." Because it was going to be slow going, we'd need every hour and would probably still get there after dark.

If we got there at all.

I looked around the cabin. "I'll throw down the

mattress so you can sleep on it tonight. And we eat the last of the food for dinner."

"We had it packed in case we need it while walking."

"Can't be helped. We eat it tonight. All of it. It's a good, hearty soup and we'll eat every bit."

"Coffee on the trail, then?"

"Lots of coffee. Every thermos filled." Coffee instead of the hot soup that would have been in them if we'd gone today.

He grinned weakly. "I love coffee." And again he apologized for hurting himself, but I ignored his words as easily as each time earlier when he'd said how sorry he was to have hurt himself in the process of trying to help.

We spent the day in front of the stove with its door open the better to watch the flames dance and flicker. I'd thrown the mattress down and it was on the floor a few feet away from the stove so we both sat on it and leaned against the pillows that were propped against the couch because the floor was easier for Jase and easier than me trying to raise him onto the couch.

I thought ahead to the morning and brought the sled inside where it would be available to simply roll him from the mattress onto it and then slide it carefully down the porch stairs and into the white, cold world that would surround us until we reached the Center.

If we reached it.

"Want to play Monopoly?" He didn't sound too enthusiastic and I knew he was merely trying to take my mind off of what lay ahead so I shook my head and lay back further into the pillows and gazed even harder into the fire so as to remember the warmth and friendliness of it during the coming day when such a memory might be all I'd have to keep me going.

Dinner was easy because the soup was already made and still warm in the thermoses but I poured it into a pan and heated it until it was near boiling and we ate it all and when we were finished the pan was as clean as if I'd washed it.

And that was the end of our food.

With the sled in the cabin, I packed it carefully, leaving space for Jase and the blankets that we'd need the last night before leaving. Then I banked the fire, closed the door to the stove, made sure Jase was comfortable and plied with aspirin, which was all we had for pain meds, and climbed to my own loft to sleep.

I didn't sleep well. I rested and slept in fits and starts between bouts of worry about the coming day during which I mentally tried every way I could think of to pull the sled in order to not wear myself out any more than necessary. Because the success of our journey, not to mention our very lives, could depend on me being able to get us to the Center.

Eventually, sleep came and when the alarm went off at three o'clock, I felt rested and ready for the coming ordeal, though where that feeling came from, I couldn't know. I do know that I prayed and prayed hard before throwing my blankets over the rail and climbing down the ladder in the dark of that very early morning, and I'm not normally a praying person outside of church.

CHAPTER 9

As I reached the main floor, I saw that Jase was awake and trying to bundle his blankets into a semblance of order and that he'd grabbed mine, too, as they'd fallen close to him. We didn't speak as we rolled them tight and tied them onto the sled. Then I made hot coffee and poured it into every thermos I could find, and we had a lot of them for fishing and forest trips and made sure the lids were tight. We dressed warmly and I pulled Jase onto the sled and headed for the door.

"Three o-clock and all's well," he said in a feeble attempt at a joke but it fell flat as I opened the door and cold air surrounded us. I'd already put out the fire so there was nothing to fight the drop in temperature. I looked around one last time, flicked on the flashlight that would be our only light until the sun came up, and then pulled the sled onto the porch.

I shut the door behind me and secured the latch so no animals would get inside while it was empty. We did that every time we left the cabin and I was determined that this time would be no different. A normal thing to do, as if this was a normal departure.

I got the sled with Jase on it down the stairs without mishap by staying on the porch and playing out the rope slowly. Jase slid nicely to the bottom unharmed and gave me a thumbs up and I slowly descended the stairs and took my first step of what would be a long and arduous journey. I hesitated because I knew what lay ahead. But after that first step, I looped the sled's rope around my waist as if I was a sled dog and set off.

I kept a slow but steady pace and discovered that it wasn't so bad. I told myself that I could do this and that was the first time I realized I hadn't been sure it was possible. But as we reached the edge of the clearing around the cabin and entered the deep forest itself, I found myself taking a deep breath.

I wanted to turn around and give the cabin one last farewell but I didn't. Instead I walked straight into the depths of the forest, following an unseen but known trail beneath the snow, kicking up clouds of white stuff with every step.

"Are you okay?" I stopped and checked on Jase. "My steps are sending snow right into your face. You must be miserable."

He shook his head. "Not at all." He held up the blanket that he was using as a shield against the snow. "It's a snow umbrella." His head tilted slightly, and I felt more than saw a smile on that granite face. "Sort of." Then, in a different tone of voice, "How are you doing? Think you can make it? You're the one doing all the work." His voice was anxious. "We just started. We can still turn back."

I moved out a little faster. "No!" The word came out like an explosion. "We are not turning back! We are going to sleep at the Center tonight!"

I kept moving.

The snow had changed everything, the whole world, and the darkness changed it even more from the forest I was used to during my walks through the woods. It was now almost unknown. I constantly flicked the flashlight this way and that just to make sure I was where I should be but, as I walked and the dark became less complete and slowly turned, instead, into a faint gray, I realized something.

I did know the forest after all. I did know where I was. I hadn't been a liar when I'd said it was my friend. I was familiar with these places and even the snow and the last vestiges of night couldn't confuse me.

With that knowledge, a strange confidence pervaded my body, sending shoots of warmth through me. The forest I'd known and loved ever since childhood was still the same. The trees hadn't turned into monsters out to snag and pull us to our doom. The huge boulders that had always been landmarks that were now buried beneath snow were still recognizable, albeit found only with the flashlight and moments spent remembering just where they were and how they were configured.

So I moved on and, after a while, I even picked up the pace a bit and just that slight increase in exertion sent additional warmth through my body, which was good because until then I'd wondered in some corner of my mind whether the warm feeling was an actual sensation or whether hypothermia was setting in and, in my semi-conscious state, I didn't know the difference between real and imaginary. But now I knew that more exertion had produced more warmth. The surety gave me added confidence.

Eventually that dark, dark, gray of pre-dawn gave

way to the lighter gray of dawn itself, though the sun remined hidden by thick evergreens. But I could see the green needles taking on a glow as the sun back-lit them. Someday, I told myself, I'd paint a picture and try to capture that subtle blur of green and gold. But not now. Now I had more important things to do.

With the rising sun came the dip in temperature that almost always comes with the advent of a winter's day, a drop of many degrees, and even as warmly dressed as I was, I could feel that chill on my face. And if I was cold, what about Jase? He wasn't walking, he didn't have the heat from exertion to warm him and he was in a veritable snowstorm caused by my kicking up the light, fluffy snow that inevitably flew back and right in his face.

I tossed a question over my shoulder, not wanting to stop because we had a long trek ahead of us and every second could be important. "It's getting colder. Do you need more blankets?"

His shout echoed from tree to tree and told me that he, too, was determined not to do or say anything to slow us down as his baritone floated cleanly through the cold air and was cheerful and confident. "I'm fine. Don't worry about me and if I fall off the sled, then you'll have easier going!"

And then he laughed and that sound, too, bounced from frozen tree to frozen tree and put a spring in my step because he'd somehow found humor in this difficult ordeal and so I laughed also, a ringing sound that would have waked any nearby sleeping bears.

Slowly the gray became true daylight and I flicked off the flashlight and looked about to make sure the night hadn't played tricks on me and sent me in the wrong direction but, no, we were right on track and at some subconscious level I thanked the forest for being my friend and showing me the way. And I continued on, carefully but surely following a path that had been laid out years before I was born, perhaps by Native Americans, or by animals seeking the easiest way from one point to another.

The forest gradually changed and a subtle downward slope told me that we were leaving the high forest where the cabin was located and heading toward the huge bog that we'd have to traverse to reach the Center, but each breath I took told me that there was no chance of it being dangerous because the below zero temperatures had surely frozen even those patches that were insulated by many years' worth of accumulated grasses. And the bog was far away, we had hours of travel before reaching it.

The sun did its warming thing and the temperature climbed a bit. Not much but the severe cold of early morning gave way to more bearable temps and the trees thinned enough that every now and then rays burst through and warmed my face and, I was sure, Jase's face, even if it had to penetrate clouds of kicked-up snow.

Warm enough that, eventually, I slowed and then stopped and removed my parka and tied it around my waist. "What are you doing?" Jase's voice was full of alarm. "It's cold out. I'm considering another layer of blankets."

I turned and for the first time since the sun came up, was able to truly see my companion. He was huddled on the sled, half lying against the packs we'd lashed to it and covered by a pile of blankets. I almost laughed. "You could be an ad for an arctic adventure, warmth guaranteed and no effort required."

"Not the arctic, please. This is far enough north for me." But he took advantage of the stoppage and tugged at the tightly wrapped blankets on the back of the sled. I dropped the rope and ran to help because I didn't want there to be any possibility of him falling off the sled and me having to somehow get him back on.

When I reached him, I removed one double mitten and felt his face. It was cold. So cold. So I slid that hand down farther to feel his chest and that was warm but not as warm as I felt was right for an injured person. Not that I know that much about first aid but being warm seemed appropriate for healing. So I took off my other double mitten and untied the extra blankets and spread them over him, tucking the sides and end in tightly enough for them not to slide off as we went.

He examined me, taking in the parka around my middle. "You still haven't told me why you're getting undressed on what must be one of the coldest days of the year."

I grinned and wondered how this man could make me smile in the direst of circumstances. But he could, and that thought warmed me even more. "Because, as I'm sure you know if you've ever been cross country skiing, exertion warms the body and it's better to shed layers than to sweat because, when you stop, that sweat will freeze to your body and you'll be in serious trouble."

"You're that warm?"

I shivered. "I will be when we get going again."

"Okay." He tipped his head to hide the frustration of being unable to walk, and I thought I saw shame in it too because a somewhat smaller than average woman was pulling him instead of the other way around. I stopped the impulse to touch his face and reassure him that I was fine with what I was doing and wondered what he'd do if I did reach out a hand and draw my fingers across his cheeks. Would he laugh or try to hide to save himself from the clutches of a mad woman? Probably both.

Then I pulled on my double mittens – his actually, being the ones he'd worn when he appeared at my door in the middle of the night -- and slid myself back in place with the rope taking the place of a dog sled harness, and moved out once more.

Then something unexpected happened but, after thinking, I realized that it was only to be expected. It was pure Jase, something that in the short time we'd known one another, I'd learned was a part of his personality that probably brought him a lot of business at the Center where I was sure patrons loved him.

He started singing. Singing! In the middle of the frozen forest on a journey that could end in disaster. He sang songs about snowflakes falling and winter wonderlands and every other winter song he could think of. And I found myself both smiling and picking up the pace because I walked to the rhythm of his singing and I wondered if that was his intent though he didn't say so.

And so we went, ever so slightly downward, and that was a good thing because it was less difficult for me and would enable me to tow Jase and the sled much faster and farther than I'd be able to on level ground. I thought ahead to the bog that would not only be level but covered with high grasses and probably drifted over. It would be hard going.

I sternly pushed the bog from my mind and wished I could sing along with Jase but knew that the effort would drain me of precious strength and that taking deep breaths of the cold air could lead to serious consequences. Jase, smothered in a cocoon of blankets, didn't have to worry about such things. So I simply listened to his cheerful, winter songs and kept moving. And smiling.

CHAPTER 10

I reached a fork in the trail. I couldn't see it for the snow that covered it like a white blanket, but I knew it was there, and I paused, thinking.

"What's wrong?" Jase's current song stopped, and a worried question came my way.

"Nothing." I pointed to the break in the trees where the path went in two directions and I pointed to the Y that led to the right. "This is a shortcut if I can remember how it goes. I know the main trail by heart but if I can get us through this shortcut without getting lost, we'll save some time." I thought about it, trying to picture it in my mind. "A lot of time but I'm not sure exactly how it goes through the forest."

He rummaged in the things on the sled. "We have the topographic map. Would that help?"

We took a break, poured ourselves some hot coffee and I read the map as I drank. Not too much coffee, I didn't want to have to stop and pee because it would take forever to remove so many layers of clothes, not to mention that it would be really, really cold. I sipped slowly and savored every bit as I examined the map. "Now I remember. I know the route and, yes, I can get us through the shortcut and save a couple of hours."

He examined me much as I'd examined the map. "What are you, anyway, some kind of forest spirit?"

"Huh?" His comment was so unexpected that I couldn't help myself.

"You know the forest so perfectly. It looked like you knew each and every tree we passed. Every trail. Every bush. It certainly seemed that way." He tipped his head back to take a healthy swig of coffee, being a guy who could pee without completely undressing, and continued. "So I know you'll get us there safely. I know it as surely as I know my name."

In a sudden bout of self-doubt so strong that I almost doubled over from it, I could only hope that he was right. But I did remember the short cut after checking it on the map and it was valid and as I studied the map the better to imprint the details in my brain, memories returned of the times I'd trekked these very paths with my dad during the summer so we could study the flora and fauna that lived near the huge bog that was so different from that near the cabin.

I'd loved the look and placement of the bog flora and fauna and in that fleeting moment I vowed that when we reached the Center and everything was fine, I'd return to the bog with pencil and sketchbook and get it all down on canvas.

When we reached the Center? What was I thinking? More like *if* we reached it. No, I told myself sternly, *when* we reached it was right. No *if* about it. I replaced the cap tightly on the thermos and shoved it back into the blankets for added insulation to keep it hot for the next time we stopped. If there was a next time. Perhaps, I told myself, I'd now simply keep going until we were warm and safe at the Center.

As I started to move, I realized that the stop had done something to me that wasn't good. During those few minutes of rest, my body, especially my legs, had grown stiff and I now had to force myself to return to the brisk pace of earlier. Plus, though I hated to admit it, the downward slope was lessening as we approached the low land and, eventually, the bog at the bottom.

I no longer swung along the trail so easily. Instead I felt each and every step until I finally warmed up once again and was able to kick snow and move myself and the sled at the pace necessary to reach the Center before full dark. Though it would be dark when we arrived, I knew that, with only brief winter daylight before night came once again, it hopefully wouldn't be the deep, black of true night, the kind of dark that made finding the way difficult if not impossible.

Jase continued singing but, as time passed and his voice went hoarse, it slowed and finally turned into a low but musical humming that kept me going as well as the songs had and then I knew that his singing was intentional because every single song had a strong rhythm and when I stepped to that rhythm the going was not only faster, it was easier. Had he been in the military that he knew how effective marching songs were? I would ask.

I wanted to stop several times and check the map but decided against it because I didn't want to lose any more time. But during one break in singing, I tossed a question back to Jase. "Think you can plot our course on the map while we move?"

"Sure." I heard rustling as he dug the map from the nest of blankets and opened it carefully so as not to tip the sled or move about, which would make towing more difficult. "Right on track," he sang out a few minutes later. "I'm amazed at how easy it is to figure out where we are." And, after a moment, with laughter in his voice, "I take back what I said about you being a forest spirit. You're just very good at reading topographic maps."

I giggled without opening my mouth because I didn't want to inhale any more cold air than necessary but was glad once again for Jase being with me because his cheerful manner made this whole ridiculous, hopeless endeavor seem possible.

Hopeless? Ridiculous? Now where had those ideas come from? We'd not ventured forth into a dangerous, freezing world without truly believing – knowing -- that we could get where we were going. Or could it be that this trip was a fantasy, merely a last desperate attempt to do something that gave us a small chance of survival over doing nothing and waiting to die?

I shivered as I shoved such unwelcome questions to the back of my mind and moved even faster along the path that I knew existed even though I couldn't see it beneath the light, fluffy snow until I was kicking up a veritable storm of white flakes into Jase's face.

"Hey," he called out and I expected to be reprimanded for too much snow in his face but I should have known Jase better than that. "We're get there in time for lunch at the rate you're going. Don't wear yourself out. Slow and steady wins the race, you know." There was a faint undertone of alarm in his voice that I ignored but I took his advice and slowed to my previous pace that I knew I could keep up for hours, and that was a good thing because hours of walking lay ahead of me. Many hours.

Jase called out for me to stop. I hesitated because once I had the rhythm down, I didn't want to break it for anything and have to get up to speed again after checking on him. But he didn't stop yelling, so I finally found a quiet place in one of the infrequent spots of sunshine where an old evergreen had crashed to the ground and new ones hadn't sprung up yet and went back to see what was bothering him.

He had something in his hand, and he held it up to me. "Lunch."

"We don't have any food, remember?"

"Yes we do." He waved his hand through the air and shoved it at me. Jerky, the kind my father kept around to snack on, but the cupboards had been empty when we left. We'd eaten every single scrap of food in the cabin. Or so I'd thought.

"It was in a drawer beside your parents' bed. Someone must have wanted it there for midnight snacks. I was going to bring it down for dinner last night when I thought better of it. I decided it would be more useful for lunch today." And once again, he shoved the jerky towards me. "It's the middle of the day, roughly, so it's time for sustenance."

I took the jerky gratefully and began to chew. Then I noticed that he didn't have any. "What about you? We share."

He shook his head hard in a way that brooked no argument. "Not today. You're doing the work, you need the calories. I'm warm and comfortable and I'm not even hungry. So eat up, lovely lady, and I'll watch and drink so much coffee that in time you'll have to stop so I can pee."

I wanted to insist that we share. To shove it down

his throat if necessary. But I didn't. I thought of the hours of walking that lay ahead and admitted that, much as it bothered me to eat while he didn't, he was right. If our survival depended on my ability to get us to the Center, then I'd best do everything possible to make that happen.

So, ducking my head to avoid seeing him not eating, I shoved the remaining jerky into the capacious pockets of my parka and returned to my place at the front of the sled, took up the rope once again, and set off.

And, yes, the jerky made a difference. As I walked and ate, I could feel energy flow into my body and I was so grateful to Jase for thinking ahead because, if it had been me, we'd have had jerky for dinner last night and nothing today.

I treated myself to jerky on a schedule. I didn't have any way of keeping track of the time beyond the sun itself and we only reached clearings occasionally to see where in the sky it was, but that was enough. Each time it moved two fingers farther towards the horizon, I'd give myself another stick of jerky. I figured that way I'd have a steady supply of fuel for my body that should last until dark. After that, if we hadn't reached the Center, I'd start praying very hard.

We had to stop once for Jase to pee. I almost laughed because he couldn't stand so had to roll halfway over to accomplish the feat and his muttered comments on his situation would have been comical if things hadn't been so dire. Actually, listening to him I decided that they *were* comical and I was grateful to Jase for once again bringing sunshine and humor into what was a very difficult situation.

When he was done, making sure he was once again tucked into blankets because he had no food to warm his body and was doing no work to turn last night's dinner into heat, and being very careful to avoid the yellow snow while doing the tucking, we once again set off.

And he started singing once again, not humming, and I found myself picking up the pace and wondered again whether he was deliberately singing tunes with a quick rhythm to get me going faster and I decided once more that when we were safe and warm I'd ask if he had military experience that included long marches in bad weather.

I checked the time. The sun was moving faster towards the horizon than I liked. Without stopping, I threw information back at Jase. "We won't get there before dark."

"That's okay," was his steady, upbeat reply. "I know the area around the Center. If you can get us anywhere close, I can guide you the rest of the way."

I found myself breathing a sigh of relief because that sinking sun had begun to worry me. I knew the way to the bog and through it but, beyond that, my father and I had never gone so I'd figured I'd have to plot a course through unknown territory using only the topographic map and how good would such a path be in the dark? Now I knew that we'd be okay if I could get us through the bog because the Center lay just beyond. Jase had said something about a path from the Center to the bog for guests to watch nature. We could follow that path.

What would we see when we reached the bog? What had the blizzard done to it? How badly had the wind blown the snow with nothing to stop it? Was it packed too hard for me to walk through but not hard enough to walk on? Had it turned the bog into a place that was so unrecognizable that I'd not know how to cross it?

As the land bottomed out and the slope turned into level ground and I knew we were getting close, I started praying that the bog wouldn't be our final resting place.

Then we broke out of the trees and it lay before us. The bog we'd have to cross in order to find safety.

CHAPTER 11

I heard Jase's indrawn breath as I stopped, and we contemplated what lay ahead. It didn't look so bad. No huge drifts to surmount, no brush thrown every which way to stop us in our tracks. Just an expanse of clean, white snow. And yet, something wasn't quite right. Something set my teeth on edge but I didn't know what it was until I took a step out of the forest and into the bog. And then I knew, and my heart sank because we couldn't make it. I knew with a certainty that lay like lead in my stomach that I could not get us across that seemingly innocent expanse.

"It's got a crust. The wind blew so hard here in the open that there's no fluffy snow anywhere. Just hard, white stuff that'll take a gargantuan effort to break through but it's not hard enough to walk on." I sank to my knees and stared at the blinding white sheet of snow that had to be traversed for us to reach the Center but that couldn't be crossed. Couldn't be.

Jase said nothing because there was nothing to say. We both stared at the bog as if wishing would change things. But it wouldn't. "I'll check out other paths. Maybe it's only hard right here. Maybe there'll be softer snow farther down." A forlorn hope but I couldn't just stand there and stare at defeat. I had to do something so I set off, one step at a time, checking the snow crust every few feet, but every time it was the same. There was no way to cross the bog.

We'd have to go around. Miles and miles more than planned and there was no way we'd make it that night. We'd have to spend the night in the forest, and it was more than likely that would be the end of us. If the cold didn't get to us, I'd simply wear out and not be able to go any further. I could feel it already, a bone-weariness that was a shadow in the background but that would grow over time until it would overwhelm me. And then all we'd be able to do was sit and wait for the inevitable.

I began to cry even though I tried not to, tears that froze on my cheeks and I didn't care because they said what I was thinking. That this was the end.

Then something happened. As I tried to shake the frozen tears away, a flash of brown swept past me mere yards away. I stopped mid-shake and followed the movement. A magnificent buck came from the forest and bounded into the bog, taking huge leaps, each yards long, as it crossed the bog we couldn't navigate as if it wasn't there, straight as an arrow and precisely where I'd have crossed if I could manage. But the buck wasn't hampered by snow because it leaped over it, hooves landing only long enough to push off again.

If only --- But I wasn't a deer so I simply watched as it disappeared into the forest on the other side of the bog.

But--- another sound made me turn back to the forest in time to see five more deer heading for the bog. No buck in this group, it was a small herd of two large, fat does, a yearling and two smaller deer that could only have been born that spring. No huge leaps for this group, no bounding across the bog as if it didn't exist. So how could they manage?

I watched.

They managed just fine. They stepped from the forest to the bog and continued on as if the crust didn't exist, heading single file in much the same direction as the buck. So how could they walk so easily through crusted snow?

As soon as the question came into my mind, the answer followed. There was a game trail across the bog, and they were walking along it single file as if the snow didn't exist. And, with a rising excitement, I realized that if they could walk along that trail, perhaps I could too.

I almost ran to the place where they'd exited the forest and sure enough, there was a game trail that went straight across the bog to the very place we wanted to go. It was deep, all the way to the ground, much too narrow for the sled but surely somehow we could manage. With renewed energy, I plowed my way back to Jase.

He'd seen the deer too and reached the same conclusion. "There's a trail. We can follow it!" He was so excited I was afraid he'd fall from the sled and we'd have a difficult time getting him back on it. "We can make it. I know we can." And only then did I know that he, too, had seen defeat as our only option mere moments earlier.

He was ahead of me thinking of how to get the sled across. He pointed to a branch on a nearby bush that was hanging and ready to fall off. "Get that branch. I can use it to push the sled and keep it on the snow." So it wouldn't slide into the narrow trail and get stuck.

"It'll be hard to keep it straight."

"I'll manage." His voice was grim. "You just get us across. I don't think it'll be as easy as it looks."

"I'm sure it won't be." But it was doable.

"There will be wind." There'd been no wind in the forest because the trees provided protection. "Look." He pointed his newly acquired branch towards the bog and so I saw the snow skittering across the hard crust like beads across ice. "At these temperatures it doesn't take much wind to turn a walk into a brutal exercise in survival." Again, I wondered if he'd been in the military but said nothing because I was too busy inspecting the bog and towing the sled to the beginning of the game trail.

We set off and Jase was right about the wind. It was worse than brutal. It took my breath away and froze the tears that wouldn't stop falling to my cheeks. I had to stop and rig a small blanket into a windbreak in order to move at all.

"We'll make it. You're doing great." He shouted in order to be heard over the wind and through the thickness of the blanket and all the clothes I wore and there was an undertone of despair in his words and I knew that I wasn't the only one who seriously doubted that we'd make it to the Center. Not today. Not tomorrow.

Not ever.

But somehow, we kept moving. I think it was the deer that did it, those five brown bodies far ahead of us that were crossing the bog just as we were. If they could do it, especially with two very young deer in the group, then we could too.

I told that to myself with every step as I ignored everything except the trail, the deer ahead that were plodding steadily along, and the snow that blew around my make-shift windbreak and into my face. My eyes. My mouth.

Once I shook my head enough to look around the blanket because I wanted to see how low the sun was towards the horizon but when I caught a glimpse of the dull red orb I wished I'd not done so because it sat exactly on the treetops. Night was coming fast. In minutes it would begin to darken, and we weren't even across the bog.

How would I see the trail? I stopped and went back, and Jase handed me the flashlight without being asked because he had seen me check the sun. I flicked it on, and the light gave me a moment of hope as it blazed and showed the trail clearer than it had been for a while because evening was coming fast and the light had been fading for a while.

But another, more insidious problem was developing. I was growing tired, so tired that each step, instead of being a cheerful movement to Jase's songs, was becoming an effort. Soon, I was afraid, no amount of effort would be enough. I took a second to look around and thought what it would be like to be stranded in the bog without even the protection of the trees when I ran out of energy and couldn't take another step.

What then?

I deliberately ignored the setting sun, the wind that still hit my face like needles, the bog itself and, instead, concentrated on the next step. One step at a time, I told myself, and eventually we'd get where we were going.

I took that one step and then I took another and another and another until the world became a blur of steps with me not knowing whether I was walking or merely thinking about walking. In some corner of my mind, I realized that was dangerous so I took a deep breath, taking in the cold air and not caring how it could chill my insides, and I gloried at the sharpness that intake of cold gave me and I looked around and realized that we were more than half-way across the bog. Within shouting distance of the other side.

So I shouted. Yelled. Told the world that I was going to sit before a fire that evening and drink cocoa and laugh as the wind blew outside. And soon Jase joined me and he, too, yelled and said whatever came into his mind and together we spooked the deer ahead of us until they sped up and ran the remainder of the distance and disappeared into the forest.

And then, after what seemed like a long time and might have been, somehow, without knowing it was happening, I stumbled and almost fell and realized that we'd reached the end of the bog and I'd struck the bank at the edge and had to climb up it and I wasn't sure I could do it but somehow I did without knowing how. Just one step at a time.

One moment we were in the bog and then we were on the bank. And then I half fell onto the sled and only Jase's arms kept me from falling into the snow. But we weren't safe yet. We still had to reach the Center.

"A break is in order," Jase said as if we weren't in dire straits and I was almost done for but, rather, as if we were walking in a park on a summer day and a bench was presenting itself for a moment's respite.

"If we stop I won't be able to get moving again," I

said, struggling to rise and start again because I was as sure as anything that stopping would be the end of us. And we were close. So close.

I felt rather than heard him nod agreement and definitely heard the muttered words that said how he wished he could take over and get us there. "We're almost there, Laurie. A couple of yards to the left you'll find a wooden walkway that leads right to the Center. If you can get the sled on it, the going should be much easier."

I struggled in the direction he pointed and found the walkway and pulled the sled onto it and started off, but it was uphill and steep and I soon knew that, close as we were, I wouldn't be able to make it even the short distance to the Center.

I was totally done, and it was dark, not quite full night but close and that blackness was the one last thing needed to put the end to what had been a good effort that wasn't good enough. Things couldn't get worse. We would die.

Then things got worse. Two eyes appeared inches from my face. I blinked and found myself staring into the eyes of a wolf. We'd got so close and now we were about to fall victim to one of the most intelligent predators in the woods.

Except Jase didn't see it that way. "Wolf!" His shout was full of gladness. "Wolf, old boy." The wolf went around me and to Jase and then the two of them became one lump as Jase hugged the wolf. Jase looked around the wolf and at me. "It's Wolf. My malamute."

A dog, not a wolf. That was small comfort though it would be nice to have company as we waited for the inevitable. A huge, strong dog with a tail that plumed over its back and muscles that rippled as it moved through the snow as if it didn't exist.

"Wolf will get us to the Center."

"How?" A nice dog, a very strong dog, but all we had was a rope and a sled, not a harness and Wolf was just one dog, not enough to pull the sled.

"Come here. Help me." Jase was digging into the pile of blankets that had kept him warm even across the brutal bog. "Do we have a knife with us? Scissors? Something that'll cut?"

There was a knife at the bottom of the pack, and I found it. As soon as he got it Jase began cutting the blanket into strips and then I knew what he was thinking. "But does he know how to pull? Won't he just sit down and do nothing?"

"We have a sled at the Center. When we have little kids there, Wolf pulls them around all by himself."

"He can't pull you, though. You're heavy."

Jase's reply was grim. "He can help. You're done in, you can't make it without help and Wolf is what we've got in the way of help and I know he'll do it if we can hitch him up."

We couldn't hitch Wolf up to the sled but we did fashion a make-shift harness that I grabbed hold of. Then I once again hitched myself to the sled, grabbed Wolf's harness and Jake told him to go ahead. "Go home, Wolf. Go home."

It took many tries before Wolf got the idea but eventually he moved out. As soon as he felt the tug on his harness, though, he sat down and looked back at Jase because this wasn't what he and Jase usually did. "Go, boy. Go home."

Wolf slowly, uncertainly, moved forward and Jase

called him all kinds of wonderful things and then Wolf got the idea that he was to pull in tandem with me and so he did. And we moved slowly up the slope towards the Center that wasn't in sight yet, but had to be close.

I cried the whole time, couldn't stop, hadn't been able to stop since that first tear in the bog. I could barely see through my tears but it didn't matter because Wolf knew the way and, if he didn't, Jase did. So we slowly, step by step, went towards warmth and safety. I didn't even try to see ahead, it was all I could do to keep hold of Wolf's harness and force a body that was already beyond its ability to keep moving.

CHAPTER 12

I almost ran into the door. I would have if Jase hadn't shouted and made me look up. "It's unlocked." Moving on automatic because I was beyond thought and knowledge of what I was doing, I opened the door and then, because it was what I'd been doing all day and couldn't think enough to know how to stop, I pulled the sled right into the main room of the Center and across the floor, stopping only when the fireplace loomed inches in front of my face.

The wind shut the door, which was good because I was beyond knowing what I was doing and I'd have left it open. Jase's voice penetrated the fog that was rapidly enveloping me. I'd kept my wits about me during the trip enough to get us here. Now I was disintegrating. "The fire is ready to go. All it needs is a match."

I didn't know what he was talking about. Fire? Match? What did they have to do with anything? I simply stood there and cried as I'd been doing since we were halfway across the bog and I kept it up now because I didn't know how to stop.

Tears ran down my face and I noted with a kind of detached interest that they weren't freezing on my cheeks and then I laughed because of course they weren't, we were inside, but that didn't make any difference, I still sobbed as if the world was ending.

I looked down. I was standing on a thick, soft rug that had probably been chosen so people who wanted to sit before a fire could be comfortable without being on chairs while making s'mores or simply watching the flames. Looking at that plush rug, one thing penetrated the fog that surrounded me. It looked like a wonderfully soft rug.

I wanted to lie down right there and then and would have if I could have figured out how to move. Then I felt Jase's hand on my leg. "Come on down, Laurie, and join me." I looked where he pretty much had ordered me to look because his voice had left no room for argument and saw him already on that rug and comfortable, having shoved the sled aside. He looked at me as if I was a freak who couldn't figure out what he was talking about, which I was because I didn't have a clue. His voice grew softer as he said, "You can stop crying now."

"I'm not crying."

"Laurie, Laurie." His voice was milk and cream and butter. "Laurie, it's okay. Forget what I said, you can cry all you want but what's important is that you can rest while you cry." He tugged on my pants leg and I found myself sliding downward and when I landed on the rug, I saw that he'd pulled the blankets from the sled and was tossing them about. Then he pulled close a couple of huge pillows put there for guests to lounge on while enjoying the fire and I just stared dumbly at him and wondered what he was doing.

"Come here," he said, reaching for me, pulling me closer, touching my face, wiping tears from my cheeks and still I didn't know what he was doing, what was happening. "It's okay, Laurie, you got me here, you took care of me, and now I'll take care of you." A warm palm rubbed my cheeks and came away wet. "Hush, Laurie, it's okay, I've got you now." And still I couldn't stop crying.

He then proceeded to remove my outer wear and I roused enough to help and then I could feel the warmth of the room that the thick clothing had blocked. I blinked. Realized at least for that moment that I was crying and tried to stop. Failed, but looked at the soft rug and the blankets through my tears and then I gave a sort of hoarse sound that meant nothing and everything and let him fold me down and place my head on one of the pillows. "That's it, Laurie. You're done. You did it. You got us here. Now rest."

He pushed me gently until I was on my side and then he covered me with blankets and tucked them around me much as I'd done for him on the sled and then the world disappeared and I knew nothing for a long time except for hearing the sound of sobbing and I'd forgotten that I was crying so I wondered who was making that racket and why didn't they stop.

Later – much, much later – I woke to find the fire blazing and Jase beside me on that rug, sound asleep and with an arm wrapped around my waist. My pillow was wet. I felt my cheeks and there were dried tears on them. Had I been crying? I couldn't remember but decided I must have been but couldn't imagine why.

Neither could I know why his arm was around me. Was he keeping me safe? Ridiculous, I could take care of myself, thank you very much, look what I'd just done, brought us both through the wilderness to safety, but the feel of that solid body spooned around me was so comfortable and warm and wonderful that I simply closed my eyes once again and turned the pillow until I found a dry spot and decided that I'd figure out later who had got the fire going and why I'd been crying and why we were on a rug instead of in bed as was proper and why he had an arm around me as if to keep me from flying away. I'd not fly away. I'd not fly anywhere. The rug was too comfortable to leave.

That masculine arm felt right -- better – different – than my father's when he'd wrapped me in safety and security when I was a child. Now I wrapped it more firmly around my waist and luxuriated in the feel and then I drifted back to sleep, only hiccupping a few times as unexpected, ridiculous sobs almost tore me apart. As sleep approached I wondered again why I was crying and I didn't know the reason any more than I'd known why I'd been crying earlier, except I must have been because my cheeks had dry tears on them and the pillow was wet.

But, even as sleep approached, I realized one thing. The fire was lovely and Jase's body next to mine was so comfortable, so secure, that my sobs were slowing until, as I lay there wrapped in comfort and warmth before that lovely fire, they finally stopped altogether and I knew that whatever my reason for crying had been, it was finished. I'd cry no more. Then I finally, truly slept.

When I woke, sun shone through the huge windows of what I now realized was the main room of the Center, with log walls everywhere, a reception counter on one side and a snack bar along the opposite wall. Chairs and small tables and couches were scattered about with, of course, the huge stone fireplace dominating the room. I was on the deep, plush rug in front of the fireplace, still covered by the blankets we'd brought from the cabin, with my head on a huge pillow meant for sitting rather than sleeping but that didn't matter, it was comfortable.

Jase was nowhere to be seen. I panicked. Could I have lost him? I racked my brain but the last part of our journey was no more than a foggy memory and I had no idea what had happened once we reached the Center. Except that the huge Malamute lying feet from me and staring at me with large, soft eyes had helped get us there, had added his considerable strength to what little remained of mine, and that his name was Wolf.

"Hi, Wolf." He wagged his tail and crawled a bit closer. "Nice doggie." Another foot or so. Did he bite? Was he friendly? He looked like a big, cuddly teddy bear. "Come here and I'll scratch behind your ears.

That did it. He scrabbled the rest of the way and when he reached me he rolled over onto his back to let me know that belly rubs were more important than being scratched behind the ears. So I rubbed his belly and he showed his appreciation with low moans of appreciation. "Good dog and thanks for saving our lives."

Another moan of enjoyment and he decided he'd had enough pampering for the moment and jumped up and began inspecting me, sniffing everywhere that wasn't covered in blankets and licking the dried tears from my face. I let him, knowing all dogs like salt and that I probably had enough on my cheeks to keep him satisfied for a long time.

Looking at the sunshine pouring through the huge

windows and feeling the love of the huge Malamute, all that crying that I now remembered faintly seemed ridiculous. And a waste of time and energy. And pathetic.

Then Wolf jumped up, ignored me completely, and ran to a door leading to some sort of inner room and woofed several times. I heard a chuckle from behind the door and recognized Jase's voice because the man was always cheerful and either laughing out loud or getting ready to laugh. I yelled, "Jase. Is that you?"

The door opened and he came out, seated on an office chair with wheels, pushing himself with his one good leg while holding his injured leg in the air. "Hi. I wondered when you'd wake up though if you slept through today and into next week that would be okay, I'd not wake you."

"It's morning." An inane thing to say but nothing else came to mind, except, "How'd you get into the chair?" He couldn't walk, after all.

"This is my home. I can do anything here." He explained. "One leg is injured but the rest of me is functional so it was merely a case of figuring out what I needed to get me around and the chair from my office would do and then to scoot along the floor until I was there and then get into the chair." He rubbed Wolf's head as the dog almost pushed him out of the chair in his eagerness to be loved. "Wolf helped in that regard. He makes a great lever."

He looked around, checked the brilliant sun, shuddered and I knew he was thinking that bright sunlight in the winter means extremely cold temperatures, and said, "Want some breakfast?"

My stomach growled. "Love some." Then I

thought about Jase in his office chair. "I'll do the cooking."

"I'm fine. I can get around in my own home."

"But you can't reach high cupboards."

He grinned and that smile rivaled the sunshine that now shone into every corner and crevice of the large room. "Yes I can. I tried so I know. I very carefully get out of the chair, balancing on one leg and then, holding onto the counter for support because I don't relish crashing to the floor, I can reach all the shelves in the kitchen." That grin grew into one of triumph. "So I ask again. Want something to eat? Bacon and eggs maybe? Or would lunch be more to your liking?"

I glanced at the old-fashioned clock on the wall with weights swinging gently beneath. "Lunch, maybe." And then I thought. "Phone calls. I should call people. Do you have a phone?"

"Of course. A landline because there are no cell towers in the forest as we well know." He looked towards the admission desk. "Whom do you want me to call and what should I say?"

"My parents, first, to let them know where I am and that I'm okay." I considered his leg and the office chair that was doubling for a wheel chair. "And then a doctor. And whoever plows the road to this place."

He nodded briskly. "Right away, but I already called the plow driver and she said she'll be here tomorrow or the day after at the latest. This wasn't the worst snowstorm in history but there are a lot of roads in the area and she knew that I didn't have guests right now so getting the Center road plowed wasn't a priority." He paused, then continued. "We have an agreement, the plow driver and me, that she'll make sure the road is clear when there are guests here but that, at other times, there'll be no hurry."

"The doctor …"

"Said that I should come in as soon as possible and that you should call him when you wake up, whenever that is, and with the skype camera, he'll ask you to examine my leg and he'll tell you what to do to keep it stable until we can get out of here." All in one breath.

I nodded and found myself relaxing once more against the huge pillow as Wolf for some reason, returned and snuggled on the blankets beside me and lay his head on my lap and Jase examined me from head to toe as best he could through the blankets that still covered me and said, "Go back to sleep, Laurie. I'll wake you when lunch is ready. Are sloppy joes okay? They are easy."

"Good idea," I said, surprised to find my words slurring as sleep once more took charge of me and I put my head on the pillow and my face in Wolf's soft fur and went back to sleep.

CHAPTER 13

When I woke next, Wolf was gone. Following the sound of a dog scarfing down food, I saw him in a small room just beyond the kitchen that was what the room behind the door turned out to be and he was gobbling down dog food – or was it sloppy joes? – and the sight and smell made me suddenly ravenously hungry. The smallish room was furnished with a large table, several chairs and a bulletin board on the wall.

Wolf stopped eating and looked at me. He must have felt me checking him out, and soon Jase came to the door also. "Wolf told me you were awake. Lunch is ready as soon as you wake up enough to move and don't worry, there's no rush because we've got all the time in the world."

My stomach said otherwise, so I quickly threw off the blankets, looked at my clothes beneath them and decided I needed a shower and clean clothes, and then I rose. That is, I started to rise. I wanted to rise. I tried to rise. I couldn't.

Then I lay back down, rolled over on one side, and by doing so managed to stand up in stages. First to my knees, then, as a chair appeared that, when I looked, was being shoved my way by a Jase who had a sympathetic and understanding expression, I managed to pull myself upright. Then I dropped gratefully into that chair. "I hurt." I held myself perfectly still. "I hurt. A lot. My whole body."

He zipped his office chair next to mine and took my hand. "Of course you do. Think what you did yesterday. You spent the entire day pulling a heavily loaded sled through a very cold wilderness and across a frozen bog. What you did would have decimated a lesser person and you can't be much more than – what? – five two?" I nodded that he had my height right. "So of course you hurt today. And you'll hurt tomorrow too." He cruised around me in that wheeled office chair and headed back to the kitchen. "When lunch is done and the dishes are in the dishwasher, if you can possibly make your way to one of the bedrooms on the main floor, I'll give you a massage."

"Can I take a shower first?"

"Of course you can and the hotter the better. Loosen those tight muscles. Give yourself a break, Laurie. You have a right to feel lousy."

"I don't have any clean clothes."

"The Center has a nice selection of lovely, expensive, white terrycloth bathrobes for guests of all sizes and shapes. Will one of them do?"

"Perfect." The thought of being enveloped in soft terrycloth made me smile over my pain. "Pure heaven."

He put a hand towards me but stopped before touching me. Consideration for my pain? "You think you hurt now? Wait until you walk more than six yards." He shrugged. "Just saying." Then he took my hand and placed it on the back of his office chair. "Lean on this and we'll get to the kitchen and lunch."

I didn't think it was possible to hurt more than I already did but I soon learned that I could and I did. But eventually we made it into the rather large kitchen that somewhat resembled a restaurant kitchen and then beyond, to the smaller room off of it, the one with the table and chairs and Wolf. He gestured. "Welcome to my employee lounge slash office and have a seat while I bring you lunch." I hurt so much that I let him serve me and I pretended that I didn't notice how much of a struggle it was for him.

Half an hour later, I pushed away from the table, full and satisfied, though still in pain and in need of a shower. "Can I shower now?"

He pointed to a second door. "Through that and first door to your right. Towels, bathrobes, and anything else you should need are waiting for you." He gulped the last of the very hot coffee we'd had with our lunch that I recognized as being from the cabin. It was high-quality coffee, I was glad he'd included it in our packs though, as I thought about it, I realized that he might have brought it so we could eat the grounds if things got really bad. Ugh!

I stayed in that shower so long and turned the water so hot that I wouldn't have been surprised if the Center ran out of hot water but it never happened and when I toweled myself dry much, much later, my body didn't hurt nearly as much as it had earlier and, when I wrapped myself in one of the luxurious terry cloth robes that lay neatly over a towel rack, I looked with distaste at my clothes in a heap on the floor. Had I actually worn those smelly things?

I opened the door and called out for Jase. "Can I wash my clothes somewhere?"

He appeared from nowhere on his magical office chair and informed me that the laundry was the room beside the bathroom so I carried my clothes there and found myself in a very efficiently laid out laundry with the largest washer and dryer I'd ever seen in a private home until I realized this wasn't just a home, this was a business that went through lots of sheets, blankets, bathrobes and much more, all of which could be found on the shelves that lined the room with neat labels. There were stacks and stacks of everything.

All Jase had to do to provide me with a bathrobe was grab an assortment of sizes from those shelves and drape them over a towel rack. I was impressed and was even more impressed when I saw the pile of blankets on the floor waiting to be laundered. They were our blankets and after being in a cabin heated by a wood stove and on a sled during the trip through the forest, they smelled both of smoke and dirt and needed cleaning as much as my clothes. Maybe more.

I added my dirty laundry to the pile and shoved them into the extra-large washer and followed the directions printed on a card taped to the machine. New hires at the Center would have an easy time learning how things worked. My admiration for Jase grew. The man was an efficient, business-savvy machine when he wasn't busy being nice and singing songs to make me march faster.

He was waiting outside the laundry when I exited and almost shoved me towards one of the several more doors along the corridor that must be the main hallway in the downstairs portion of the Center. He called out 'stop right there' when I was about to pass a door and told me that was my bedroom for the duration of my stay and then he reminded me that he'd promised me a massage.

"I'm not a professional but I know which muscles are most likely to hurt."

"Were you in the military?" At last I'd find out where he'd learned about marching and, evidently, about sore muscles.

"I was in the Army long enough to visit Afghanistan and decide the military life wasn't for me. When I got out after that one enlistment, I looked at a map for the most un-military place I could find and this was it and I've never regretted that decision."

"Did you march a lot in the Army?"

"Too much." So that answered my question.

His hands did magical things to my sore muscles and his voice did even more magical things to my mind and soon I was floating in a void of sensation and an imaginary world that included sloppy joes and wonderful dogs and snow and a man who'd arrived in the middle of the night in a blizzard and, strangest of all, of lovers. They all featured prominently in my daydream and I wondered when I'd stop thinking of Jase and lovers and snow and wonderful dogs and decided that the answer was probably never.

Lovers? I knew where that imagery came from. We were a couple through necessity, though not lovers, and would remain so until he saw a doctor and got something done to his leg so he wouldn't have to scoot about on a wheeled office chair. Thinking about that chair reminded me that I was supposed to call his doctor and I decided to do just that as soon as his strong, magical hands finished turning what had started out that morning as a mangled piece of painful flesh back into me.

By the time he was done massaging away the pain, I was asleep once more and he let me sleep, pulling the huge quilt that covered the bed over me and quietly shutting the door. I don't know how long I slept but when I woke, I felt like a new person, full of fuel and limp with relaxation, and the sun was decidedly low in the small spot of sky visible through the window close to the bed.

I considered the view. Evergreens, of course, because this was the north woods, and a sky full of white, wispy clouds, plus that winter sun with its thin but brilliant light. Must be cold out, I decided without caring one way or the other because I was warm and comfortable in a huge bed in a large building that was built specifically to cater to a visitor's every whim. At the moment I was that someone and the feeling was so luxurious that I wanted to roll over and sleep some more.

But I didn't because Jase's doctor might not take callers at night and the sun was dropping fast and his leg needed attention. So I shoved off the quilt and slid out of bed, surprised to find that I could pad barefoot to the door with only minor pain, and then I went looking for Jase.

"We must call the doctor," I said without preamble. "It's late."

He nodded and dialed a number from the phone book beside the land line. It was already open to the right page so, as he'd patiently waited for me to awaken, he'd also been keenly aware of the passing time.

The doctor's office answered on the second ring

and soon we were on speakerphone with the doctor himself, which was when I discovered that Jase had already booted up his computer and pulled up Skype while I was still a quivering, painful mass of tired flesh. And now they were ready for a medical consultation that would somehow involve me.

"Jase," the doctor said in that competent voice doctors have, "either skinny out of your pants or cut off the pants leg so I can see your injury."

"No way am I going to destroy a perfectly good pair of jeans," was Jase's reply and before I knew what was happening, he was unsnapping those jeans and wiggling out of them. I didn't know whether to enjoy the show or look away but neither was necessary because he wore nice, white, cotton undershorts that could easily have passed for swimming trunks. So I forgot to be embarrassed and, along with the doctor on Skype, I examined his leg.

It was a mess and that mess extended from his hip to his toes. Bruises were beginning to show and everywhere I looked the leg was swollen. I couldn't figure out a single thing by looking but to the doctor, all those bruises and swollen places meant something. "Feel his leg, will you, Laurie? Not too hard, mind you, we don't want to send him into shock, but the first thing I need to know is whether anything is broken."

I felt somewhat competent about that because I'd done much the same thing in the shed when I found him and soon the doctor agreed with my original diagnosis that he'd not broken any bones. "That's good, but it appears that he has extensive soft tissue damage." He peered closer at his Skype. "Jase, I believe you insulted just about every muscle, ligament, and joint in that leg and the sooner you can get in here for me to see it in person the better," He looked from the leg to us. "Now? Can you come in now? I'll stay late if need be."

Jase explained that the road wasn't plowed. The doctor nodded quickly as if he'd heard that before. "As soon as possible, then." He pursed his lips. "Does Maude plow your roads?" When Jase assured the doctor that she did, he smiled. "I'll get hold of her. Tell her to get your road clear ASAP and she'll get to you pronto. Tonight if she's not on the other side of the county at the moment, tomorrow morning if there aren't sick, injured, or pregnant people on her route who are in worse shape than you."

"I'll have coffee ready when she comes. And cookies or something else that's equally sweet."

The doctor snorted. "You'd better or she'll let you know that you've been placed on her plow-last list. I hear her granddaughter is riding with her so that's double reason to have sweet treats." And he wiped his glasses clean, reached for the button on his computer, and winked out of existence, after which Jase shut off his computer, too, and we were left to prepare dinner because during our talk with the doctor, that brilliant, bright sun had also winked out of existence and night had arrived and it was time to eat. Again. It seemed as if I'd just finished lunch instead of sleeping away the afternoon after sleeping away the morning.

One non-existent day except for the luxurious shower and massage. I closed my eyes to better remember them and followed Jase on his office chair slash wheelchair and wondered what was for diner.

CHAPTER 14

I helped fix the meal and, in so doing, learned how the Center kitchen functioned, filled as it was with stainless steel tables and other kitchen-type equipment that I recognized but had never seen on the scale that the Center obviously required. What I soon learned in my awe-struck way was that it worked very well and soon we had steaks and broccoli from the freezer cooked and on the table, steaming and giving off wonderful smells. A couple of bananas and mashed potatoes made from a box completed the meal and it came together so quickly that I realized Jase was a master in the kitchen. He'd make some woman a wonderful husband.

We ate at that table beneath the bulletin board while Wolf gobbled down his dog food nearby. It was a lovely meal and the errant thought went through my mind that this was as enjoyable as any restaurant meal I'd ever experienced. Did kitchen staff at restaurants have it better than the patrons they served?

The snowplow was delayed by two days because a pregnant woman went into labor three weeks early and the parents-to-be followed the plow all the way to the hospital because Maude, whoever she was, wouldn't take any chances on the anxious couple getting stranded on the way. Then a man at the other end of her route developed stomach pains that had him doubled over and the doctor diagnosed possible appendicitis so Maude once more went to the rescue and, of course, wouldn't leave the man and his wife who was driving with hands clenching the wheel in concern, until they were safely in the hands of the Emergency Room people.

Then she plowed her way to the Center and rescued Jase with her granddaughter at her side enjoying the ride and the break from school that I suspected wasn't official but was, rather, the kind of break families give their kids to educate them beyond what's in books and to have fun in the process. Kate, the granddaughter, insisted that when she grew up, she was going to plow roads in the winter and grade them in the summer just like her grandmother.

Kate watched with interest from the window of the plow as her grandmother scraped snow from everywhere, not stopping until the Center could be accessed as easily in winter as in the middle of summer. Then both grandmother and granddaughter come inside and the granddaughter, Kate, followed her nose to the several dozen cookies cooling on newspaper on one of the several counters in the spotless kitchen. I was proud of myself. I'd made the cookies, cookie baking being the one culinary skill I possess.

Maude grabbed cookies and milk for Kate and more of each for herself and as she poured she breathed in the fumes and then breathed out a smile that said she knew good coffee when she smelled it, and they made their way to the stainless steel table against the wall in the careless way people do who are repeating a well-known routine.

Jase and I joined them and soon I was treated to a gossip fest, except it wasn't exactly gossip as I quickly learned. There were no negative comments nor were there any judgements. Just facts and more facts. The woman was a living, breathing newspaper and knew everything that was going on in the community because she watched and listened as she plowed and graded and scraped and, since she kept all the roads in the county drivable plus also plowing most of the driveways, she covered a lot of territory and at almost every crossroad or house she stopped for coffee and chit-chat and was welcome everywhere and, therefore, knew everything -- absolutely everything -- that was happening in the entire county.

The Johnsons had decided not to get a divorce after all and were trying to work things out. Maude carefully made no judgement on their chances but Kate nodded sagely and said they were nice people.

Carrie Lee was engaged, and everyone was surprised because it wasn't to her long-time boyfriend but, rather, someone she met at college and the former boyfriend was okay with the whole idea because he'd moved on, too.

Carter Lee, Carrie's grandfather, had put his farm up for sale and when it sold, he'd move into town. Close to stores and people. Good move on his part. Maude approved.

Maude was tall and robust but she was still a woman doing a man's job and I couldn't help but be curious about her and, though I thought I hid my curiosity well, it turned out that she read me like a book and eventually, with the kind of expression that said this happened every time she met someone new, answered my unasked question. "I got in the business when my no-good husband left me and the kids for a waitress from a café in the next town over."

She snorted as she repeated what I'd figured out by then was a frequently told story. "When he sent me a letter giving me legal ownership of all that expensive equipment so I could sell it so he and his lady love could live the good life, I didn't do exactly what he wanted."

She laughed and Kate laughed with her, settling in with a grin to hear what must be a familiar and enjoyable story. "I took that letter to my lawyer who said it gave me the equipment but didn't expressly say I had to sell it and give the money to him. So I didn't. Instead, I went outside and stared at those machines and figured out how to operate them and I've been doing it ever since and from what I hear, he and his lady love are working their tails off to make ends meet." She snorted her appreciation for the way justice had prevailed and her granddaughter echoed that snort and then nodded her head several times, ponytail bobbing.

Then little Kate sat up even straighter. It was clear that she couldn't be prouder of her grandmother and almost strutted as she and Maude finished their drinks and cookies and left. Coming after them, I helped Jase into his truck and we followed them to the highway where Maude waved us towards town because she knew we'd have clear roads from then on as she and her granddaughter went one way and we went the other, into town and straight to the medical clinic.

The waiting room had the usual stack of out of date magazines and I learned a lot about what had been happening in the world a year ago as I waited for Jase after he'd been deposited in a wheel chair and whisked back to some unknown location. Time must not be important in the north country because surely they were back there having a great old time when the doctor returned, followed by Jase with a pair of crutches that gave him the jaunty look of an injured soldier. Had he been wounded in Afghanistan? I'd have to ask.

The doctor looked about until he saw me. He led Jase to my corner of the waiting room and spoke. "Good thing Jase here has you because he's not going to be using that leg for a long time. Weeks. A couple of months. Maybe more." He scowled in a doctor kind of way and continued. "No broken bones, just as we surmised, but he either strained, sprained, pulled, or tore everything in his entire leg that it's possible to mess up and that's a lot."

It was a good thing that he had me? Really? I cringed because he didn't have me, exactly. We barely knew one another. But I said nothing. Instead I stared at the crutches and Jase's leg now encased from hip to toes in what I later learned was a leg immobilizer because, with no broken bones he didn't need a cast. And I made a decision.

I was here, I had no pressing schedule, and he needed help. I could provide that help. I nodded agreement to everything the doctor said. "No driving, of course, wrong leg, if he'd have done that to his left leg he'd be able to drive in a couple of weeks, but not with all that damage to his right leg."

He tut-tutted as if Jase should have chosen which leg he wrecked and then he handed him a prescription. "Pain killers if you need them, though if you've gone this long without them you will most likely throw the prescription away. But I suggest you fill it because they might be handy to have around in case that leg decides to act up later on." And then to me. "Bring him back in a week and I'll see how things are coming."

The crutches made a big difference. Jase got to the truck under his own power and even insisted on accompanying me into the drug store to get the prescription that he'd probably not take filled and then we stopped for a pizza lunch at Jerry's where he told the story of our miraculous journey through the winter forest and across the bog to everyone who would listen. Which was everyone.

"She got us through." He pointed to me and they all nodded. "The woods weren't so bad and she's got a thing with the forest, a connection, as if they are buddies or something and the forest won't let anything bad happen to her.

"But she also towed me on a sled across the bog and that was a whole different thing." You could hear the collective indrawn breaths because everyone there knew the bog and so knew how dangerous winter winds could be across its open swaths. "She's a hero.'

One elderly gent nodded agreement and said somberly, "Lots of heroes around here. Have to be to live in the north country but that doesn't lessen what she did. I'd hate to cross that bog in winter pulling a sled."

His companion, a somewhat younger man, possibly his son, added, "She's a little thing, too, Amazing that she could pull a big guy like you and all the things you'd need to bring with you."

A third person, a youngish woman, asked, "What

are you going to do now? Didn't you say her car is at the cabin and that there's a perfectly good snowmobile somewhere in the forest?"

Everyone waited for our answer. Jase licked his lips for a moment before answering. "We haven't thought that far yet but of course we'll get the snowmobile. We can use another snowmobile and tow it back." He raked his hair, leaving it spiking every which way. "As for the car, we'll have to see if Maude has time to plow out the road to the cabin. It's not on her winter route so it'll likely depend on whether any more storms come this way because, if they do, she'll be too busy to bother with one little car."

He hunched his shoulders as he looked at me and it was only then that I realized I might be without personal transportation until spring. I closed my eyes as I thought how to get around without a car when Jase was better.

I decided that once Jase was okay to be on his own, if Maude couldn't plow out our cabin and I somehow returned to Minneapolis I could use public transport but I'd have to get there first and Jase couldn't drive me because he couldn't drive and, anyway, then I'd be stranded in the city until spring and even then I'd have to ask my parents to drive me to the cabin so I could get the car and what if it wouldn't start after all that time buried in a snowdrift?

I groaned as I contemplated all the problems inherent in a tiny car beneath a pile of snow beside a wilderness cabin on a road that wasn't on anyone's plow route. The entire room groaned with me because they understood the intricacies of life in the north woods in winter.

Then we finished our pizza and Jase swung jauntily to the truck on his new crutches that he was mastering as I watched and I drove back to the Center on roads that were as clear as in the summer thanks to Maude. The county had lucked out when her husband deserted her because she was very good at what she did.

Once at the Center, Jase, the man with a smile that never dimmed and a good word for everyone all the time suddenly and unexpectedly turned grouchy. I didn't understand it and watched warily as he stared at the land line phone as if it were a snake that could bite him until finally, moaning without realizing he was doing so and that I could hear him, he picked up the receiver and riffed through a rolodex of phone numbers and began dialing.

He looked at me and mouthed, "I'll find someone to come and help me." I hadn't told him of my intention to be that help and I decided to wait and see whether he could find help himself. Then I could somehow get home and get on with my life.

He shook his head in frustration as he waited for someone to pick up. "I need help at the Center, and I need it soon," he muttered as he hung up the phone, consulted his rolodex and dialed another number. "I have a group coming in a little over a week and then there will be at least two more groups this winter, way before I'm functional. More if some pending reservations are firmed up."

My mouth dropped open. He had a business to run, I'd not thought about that, and doing so involved doing things he couldn't do without two good legs. I was glad I'd not made my offer out loud because what did I know about running an event center?

He continued, thinking as he spoke. "I can do the inside stuff. Cooking, cleaning, laundry, and I can handle some decent fireplace chats and organize games in the great room." He shook his head. "But outside?" He stared malevolently at his messed-up leg. "I can't lead a group of snowmobilers. Even though we stick to groomed trails, I must be able to help if anyone has trouble and, as you can clearly see, I can't do that with a bum leg. I could give directions to a helper but I need someone to be that helper."

He started ticking off a list of things he couldn't do while injured and his face took on an almost glazed look of panic. "Nor can I lead anyone on cross-country ski trips. Or do the outside work to have a picnic in the snow."

"You have picnics in the snow?"

"Of course." As if everyone had snow picnics. "They are wonderful. All the good food you can imagine, a roaring campfire, hot cocoa, s'mores, and no mosquitoes. They are one of the highlights of every stay, the thing guests talk about when they tell people of their winter getaway."

Then he ignored me as, with a sigh that said he didn't expect much, he started dialing the phone and I didn't even ask permission to use the kitchen and prepare dinner. I just went and looked to see what I could make because I wasn't about to endure that frown that I imagined grew as he spoke to one person after another after another.

I found some pork chops and enough things to go with them to call it a meal and wondered whether I should tell him dinner was ready or simply wait until his phone calls were done and he'd hopefully found someone to help out, after which he'd once again become his usual smiley self.

CHAPTER 15

Considering the grumpy voice in the other room, staying in the kitchen seemed the best option so I turned on the ceiling fan and waited for the smell of dinner to draw him there and eventually, about the time my stomach was rumbling so badly that I was ready to eat without him, he came. One look at his face said he'd not been successful.

"Did you find anyone?" I pretended not to know how the phone calls had turned out, feeling somewhat lost as to how to proceed because, until now, there'd been no need to be diplomatic with Jase. Until now he'd been the diplomat and I'd blurted out whatever I felt like saying.

He sank into the empty chair at the table and I scurried to get him a plate of food though he'd gotten his own before then. This action on his part must mean things were really bad and it turned out that I was right. "No luck." He shook his head as if he couldn't believe his lack of success. "Everyone is either busy or has gone south for the winter." In his voice was surprise that anyone would leave the wonderland of the north woods in winter. Then he said it again. "No one at all. I'll have to close the Center."

I took a deep breath and wondered if I'd hate myself later for what I was about to say. "I don't have to be back at any particular time. I can stick around for a while."

His eyes raised to mine. "Really? Don't you have a job you must get back to?"

I scowled because I'd heard this refrain many times because few people believe artists can make a living with their art. "I'm an artist. Painting pictures *is* my job and I can and do set my own schedule."

Something appeared in the back of his eyes. A light. A hope. But his words were carefully spaced as he slowly asked, "Don't you have a studio somewhere where you work?"

Did I? I laughed, picturing my so-called studio. "I'm a professional artist to the extent that I don't need a day job but –" I took a deep breath and decided to be honest. "But the reason I don't need a second job is that I live in a tiny, cramped, one-room apartment that doubles as my studio."

I closed my eyes and mentally counted the half-finished pictures that littered that room. "I can't have company because there's no place for them to sit. Or walk. Or even stand and I pretty much crawl around and over pictures and equipment to get wherever I need to be." Cooking was a challenge.

That light – the hope -- in the back of his eyes grew as he cut his pork chop into precise, square pieces and took a bite. Precise as in matching his thoughts? His next words didn't clarify anything as he asked, "Is your studio portable?"

"Huh?" The question was the last I'd expected, and I was clueless as to his reason for asking except that he clearly had an idea and he was approaching it sidewise and slowly. Inch by inch.

"I mean, can you only paint in your apartment? Your studio? Whatever you call it?" He scratched his head and frowned because he was treading as lightly around me now as I'd been doing around him earlier, which meant that he didn't want to mess up whatever he was up to. Which meant it was important. "I don't know anything about artists but I'm guessing that creativity is fickle." Another head scratch and hunched shoulders. "I guess what I'm trying to ask is whether you can only paint in your apartment or can you be creative in other places?"

My relief was so great that I laughed. "I'm the opposite of fickle. I paint wherever I happen to be. In my apartment, in the cabin, in the forest. Anywhere and everywhere."

His sigh of relief filled the room and mingled with the aroma of pork chops and applesauce as that light – that hope -- in the back of his eyes spread until his entire face glowed. "Do you think you could paint here? At the Center?" I blinked because I was still clueless. "And maybe do a few other things between pictures?"

Oh! A glimmering of his thoughts appeared. I swallowed applesauce and changed my mindset to parallel his, wondering if later I'd wish I'd kept silent. "Please explain in a bit more detail." I stuck my nose slightly into the air because I was scared for what I was about to commit to and didn't want him to know.

His eyes drifted up and down my body, head to toes as if he'd never seen me before but it was done without meeting my eyes. He was trying to gauge my feelings as I'd tried to gauge his after his marathon phone session. Which was odd because we knew each other well after our short acquaintance, though I supposed that in life or death situations that was common, and this was different so in a way we were strangers once again. This situation involved the making of decisions.

He lay down his fork and knife and looked me straight in the eyes. "What I'm wondering – okay, what I'm hoping – is that you'll consider sticking around for a while. Staying at the Center until I'm back on my feet." He gazed at his leg all neatly wrapped and sticking out one side of the table. "Literally."

He waved a fork, dug into those small, square pieces of pork chop, staring at them as if wondering how they'd gotten cut into such tiny pieces. "There are three bedrooms on the main floor of the Center. They are for the Center owner and the manager and his family. That's me since I'm both owner and manager and I only need one bedroom. You are now in the second bedroom and if you agree to stick around it'll be yours indefinitely. That leaves one entire bedroom that could be converted into a studio."

We stared at one another for a long time without speaking as I sucked in my breath and tried to wrap my mind around the fact that I'd done it. I'd agreed to stay and now, if I chose, I'd agree to help out indefinitely and bring my art things to the Center, which would be a huge thing. I asked, "Does that third bedroom have a north window?"

He stared at me as if I'd lost my mind so I continued. "North windows provide indirect light and that's important for painting." The one good thing my tiny apartment had was a huge north-facing window. It looked out on another apartment building several yards away, but it did face north.

He blinked. Thought. Tilted his head a bit. And smiled. "I believe it does." He rose and grabbed his crutches. "Let's go see." As he reached the door leading to the bedrooms, he put one hand into a cabinet and pulled out a compass and waved it about. "Comes in handy when I'm in the woods." Then he thumped down the hallway and I followed, wondering if I was insane and what I'd say if the bedroom did, indeed, have a northern exposure because then I'd have no way out.

I was so deep in thought that it's amazing that I didn't bump into him as he reached his destination and paused long enough to push open the door to a spacious room that was most likely intended as the master bedroom. It was beautiful. And large. And had a wall of windows overlooking the forest mere yards away that undoubtedly, definitely, amazingly faced north.

I didn't need confirmation from his compass to know because I recognized the indirect light that filtered through the trees and into the room. Any artist knows that light. As I looked around, I realized that this was perfect, down to the bathroom across the hall that could be used for cleaning myself and any mess I might make, and I make a big mess.

I said the first thing that came to mind, as if my decision was already made. Which, in a way, it was. "We'd have to cover the floor with something. Drop cloths or old rugs." I flushed. "I'm kind of messy and I'd hate to stain these lovely wood floors."

He waved a hand in the air as if stains were nothing, holding his crutches to his body as he did so, which showed how much of a crutch expert he already was. "Drop clothes. Rugs. Blankets. Whatever. It can be done. Whatever you need can and will be done, though you might have to do it yourself if it's something I can't manage."

As relief flowed from every pore of his body and he realized that possibly his crisis could be handled, he added, "We can work out the details in the kitchen as we finish that lovely dinner you prepared that I'm afraid I didn't notice."

"It'll need to be re-heated."

Another wave of that arm. "Whatever." Then worry returned, creasing his forehead. "Surely we can work out any problems. Can't we?" And grimly, "I hope we can because frankly, Laurie, you are my last hope. If for any reason you can't do this, then I'm going to have to cancel a whole lot of reservations and I don't know if the business can stand the loss and that's the honest to goodness truth."

We returned to the kitchen silently, each thinking our own thoughts, and I warmed up the dinner I'd made and knew that the re-heated food wouldn't be as good as when it was first cooked, but knowing that wasn't important. The only thing that mattered was whether we could come to an agreement on my future at the Center and, as I thought about it, there were a lot of things to consider.

Like what would I be doing, exactly? If Jase could only do things inside, that seemed to mean that I'd be doing a lot of stuff outside and was I up to it? Could I do those things? What needed doing outside?

The first item on his agenda wasn't chores, it was money. "How much will you charge to work for me?" I giggled because the question seemed backwards.

Usually an employer tells the future employee what they'll receive.

I thought about it. "Nothing because if you include board and room, my expenses will be less here than in Minneapolis and I'll still get income from the pictures that I'll paint here." And I'd have a beautiful studio to work in.

"Are you sure?"

That light in his eyes showed that he'd not figured paying full-time help into his financial calculations so my decision was appreciated. I assured him that I meant every word. "But I need to know what will be expected from me and that I'll have time to paint."

I looked out the window at the piles of snow the plow had made around the parking lot. "All those outdoor things you mentioned. Maybe I'm not up to the task. There are things I don't know how to do. Lots of things." Things that my father had always done because he was the outdoor type while my mother cooked and I meandered through the woods and painted.

He scowled as if he'd not thought that far ahead. Then he brightened. "If you can drag a sled full of equipment that also has me on it through the wilderness for a full day, then you can do anything. I know you can."

"I was worn out at the end of the day. So exhausted that I was out of it."

"I remember." He nodded somberly and let his hands drop to the table. "You were crying before we reached the Center and didn't stop until almost daylight the next morning. I didn't know what to do. I was terrified." We both were silent.

"But that was different, we were in a life-

114

threatening situation and that was your reaction to it. The thing that's important right now is that, even though you cried, even though you were at the end of your rope, even though you thought you couldn't do it, you kept going. You kept walking. You did it. You got us here."

He reached across the space between us and touched my face, drawing a hand along my cheek as he'd done once before only this time there was compassion and more in that motion, and I asked, "Were you wounded in Afghanistan?"

The question was so unexpected that it broke the tension and he laughed. "Only if being hit by a ball during a game of baseball counts." He sobered. "But I learned how to run when the bombs came. Fast."

I laughed too as my stomach turned over at the thought of what he'd experienced, and somehow I knew that we'd be able to work out the details, whatever they might be and I knew as surely as I knew my name that I was about to become an unpaid but important employee of the Center.

CHAPTER 16

There were a lot of details. A lot of outdoor things that I'd be doing and most of them were things I kind of knew how to do but wasn't a professional in. Like snowmobiling.

"You'll lead groups."

"I can ride a snowmobile but I'm not proficient."

"It'll all be on groomed trails and you'll take the lead and go as slow as you wish." He grinned, an uplifting of his lips that added depth to the light in his eyes. "The rides are advertised as a 'Winter Wonderland Sightseeing Trip' so if anyone gets ideas about racing or other unwise activities, I call them to account and make them slow down."

My grin matched his. He knew how to control a situation. "So no one goes fast on snowmobiles around here?"

He tipped his head and those eyes twinkled. "Only if they bring their own snowmobiles that they take on unsupervised trips, which they can do and my insurance isn't involved if they crash and burn." His expression returned to normal. "We can go for a ride today if you like. You drive and I'll ride shotgun." He thought more. "There are trail maps and, of course, you have your topographic map if you want to use it."

It sounded doable. Sort of. "What else besides snowmobiling?"

He ticked off a list on one hand. "Cross-country skiing, also on groomed trails and with much the same rules. Snowman and snow fort building if the temperature is right for making snowballs."

"Are there ever snowball fights?"

"Always."

"Okay. What else?"

"Anything snow-related and, of course, there'll be the picnic in the snow that the Center is known for. I'll do the catering and will be there on a lawn chair to talk to everyone but you'll have to get everything ready and be available for whatever people might need."

I found myself nodding. He continued, "When we take that snowmobile ride to get you acquainted with it, we can cut across country as I did when I ended up at your cabin, and tow the broken snowmobile back and pick up anything at the cabin that you might want to bring here."

I looked down at my clothes, the same ones I'd worn since leaving the cabin. Why hadn't I thought to bring something to change into? Because I hadn't expected to succeed? "Clothes would be nice." Lips that were pressed hard together to avoid another grin said my reply was what he'd expected, as he said, "That'll be tomorrow. Tonight we have a marshmallow roast in the fireplace in the great room and we practice making s'mores and staring into the fire."

"Is that also on the agenda?"

"Absolutely, but as it's an indoor thing, it'll be my domain. But it'll be good practice because guests will expect both of us to be in attendance whenever possible because we will be the host and hostess." Host and hostess. The words had an unfamiliar ring.

The fire that evening brought back the fire that first night, when someone – Jase – had got it going and I'd simply stared into the flames and warmed myself on that thick, comfy rug. Now s'mores were added, and the evening lasted far too long. It was way past midnight when we reluctantly tamped down the fire and retired to our bedrooms.

But before I went to bed, I found myself going past my bedroom door in order to check once again the room that would become my studio. It was large and filled with bedroom furniture but in my mind it already held the totality of my paintings and equipment.

The next morning, we got going right after breakfast, maps in the glove compartment of the snowmobile, along with ropes and packs to carry things back with. The trip was gorgeous, the trail wound among some of the most beautiful stretches of forest in the area and skirted the bog that had almost been our undoing. Now it lay before us as an interesting piece of northern territory instead of a foe to be overcome.

A small herd of deer crossed as we watched, using the trail the buck had used and the does and younger deer, the trail that had saved our lives. We watched until they disappeared in the woods on the other side and then we went on our way.

The broke-down snowmobile was a white lump but it was easy enough to brush off the snow and tether it to the one we rode, and then we continued through the pristine forest to the cabin, where I packed everything I'd brought with me for our Christmas vacation, plus all the gifts I already had packed in the car, plus the portrait of Jase that I'd started. Now I would get a chance to finish it.

Unpacking things from the car required brushing snow off until my tiny car once again was recognizable, though as I emptied it of packages, I realized once more that there was no way such a small vehicle could get anywhere in the amount of snow that the blizzard had dropped.

Then we slowly and carefully returned to the Center, where Jase went inside at my insistence and I pulled the damaged snowmobile onto a trailer to bring to town for repairs because, though Jase could normally fix it himself, he chose not to have me do the work with him giving instructions.

"You have enough to worry about learning the things you need to know. Let someone in town takes care of this beast." Another expense. I was glad I'd made the decision to stay and help and not ask for wages. He was too nice a person to lose his business because of a bum leg.

Over dinner that night, one he fixed while singing at the top of his lungs and hobbling around the kitchen with verve on a pair of crutches, he approached another thing he'd need help to accomplish. "Tomorrow is Sunday. I'd like to go to church if you don't mind driving."

"Sure." I flushed. "I'm afraid I'm not as good at attending church as I should be. This will be a chance to remedy that flaw."

"Me neither, usually, but after what we went through and survived, I'd like to check into God's place and tell Him thanks for saving our lives."

I thought. "The buck showed us that there was a path and a small herd of deer showed us where that path was."

He continued. "And Wolf was where we needed him right when we needed him to be there."

"Coincidence?"

"Maybe. Maybe not."

I took a long swig of milk. "I think I'll give thanks too."

"Just in case it wasn't the biggest coincidence in history." He looked at the floor and his voice was husky. "We shouldn't have survived, I realize it now that I can look back on that day." But we did survive and now Jase wanted to do the right thing. So I put my hand on his and we let our glances meet for a moment as we gave thanks that we were alive.

Church the next day was small and filled with people. The sermon was probably good but I didn't hear a single word because I was busy silently saying 'thank You,' over and over again and I wished it had lasted longer because when it was done I wasn't sure I'd given thanks enough times. Then we adjourned to a largish room for fellowship, which consisted of coffee, three kinds of cookies, where a throng of people wanted to hear the story of our miraculous trip through the forest that Maude had spread through the county. Everyone had a comment or an opinion.

"Can be done, I know that, but not many people would even attempt it."

Jase gulped his coffee, not as good as that from the cabin that was now the Center's preferred blend, but it was hot. "You have to understand. Laurie is special."

"How so?" Eyebrows rose.

"She has this thing with the forest." He'd said it before. Now he said it again as he brushed crumbs from his lap. "Yes, she's good at reading maps but I think she'd do okay without them because she knows the forest. She lives and breathes to the same rhythm as the forest. She could do it and I knew she could, that's why I pushed for going to the Center, because I recognized what she is. She's – special. A kind of snow queen."

A few heads nodded as others turned to me as if trying to see what Jase saw. There were shrugs and more nods and then everyone turned back to their conversations and cookies.

An elderly man said, "That bog, though. That's a killer." This time everyone within hearing distance agreed and a shiver went through me at the realization of what could have happened. I said a few more 'thank Yous' and finished my coffee and cookies and stood up and then Jase and I left and returned to the Center, silent and thoughtful and every so often I'd find my gaze going skyward but all I saw were small, white clouds scudding across a China blue winter sky.

When we arrived at the Center, Jase declared that tomorrow we'd have a picnic.

"Outside?"

"Of course. It'll be fun and instructive, and I'll get everything ready so all you have to do is decide what you need done in the third bedroom. There's a handyman I call every so often. He'll come and get the present furniture out and maybe even go with you to Minneapolis to bring whatever you need back." He continued. "I want it done as soon as possible just in case you're thinking of changing our mind." He licked his lips. "You have no idea how essential you are about to become. I need you here so I want to cut off any possibility of retreat."

The next day, there was no wind and the sun was as warm as a winter sun can be, which wasn't very warm but I was dressed in many layers and the fire that I started in the large, metal ring under Jase's instructions eventually had me unzipping my parka and removing my mittens.

Jase showed me where to find dinnerware that I put on the large table beside the outdoor grill and he cooked us a sumptuous feast that we ate on logs surrounding the fire that doubled as stools. As we ate, I decided that food was a large part of why people returned to the Center year after year.

Jase grinned and explained. "I like to cook."

"And I like to eat." I looked at the setting sun. "What's it like having a picnic when it gets dark?"

"We have the fire going. Some groups prefer eating late, under the stars. What say we come back when it's dark and make s'mores?" I was learning that s'mores were a fixture at the Center.

Were s'mores on their advertisements? I decided to ask when I'd been there long enough to have a say in such things. If I was there long enough for anything beyond Jase's healing.

Between the outdoor picnic and the outdoor s'mores party, Jase contacted the handyman, Petra, who said he'd be there bright and early the next morning to drive me to Minneapolis and move everything I wanted into that third bedroom. After he'd removed the current furniture, of course.

Jase asked if he could ride along. "A chance to get some things for the Center." He scratched his head, a gesture I'd come to realize was typical Jase. "Specialty stores are great but shipping sometimes makes me think twice. But if you'll be going to the city, I'd like to go along and take advantage of the ride."

I panicked. I'd have to know by tomorrow what I wanted brought back to the Center of all the things in my over-crowded apartment. I didn't know and wouldn't know until we got there, and I could look over my cluttered apartment-slash-studio. So I didn't enjoy the s'mores as much as I might have in spite of the fact that the stars and moon were out in full glory and there was no wind and the fire that we'd stirred up and thrown more logs on snapped and crackled and lit up the dark with a red glow that would scare any wild animals away and welcome any people who happened along.

I did notice that the s'mores were delicious. Why hadn't I had any since childhood? Why had I thought of them as just a kid thing? I stuck another marshmallow on my stick, leaned back comfortably against a log, and watched as it turned just the right shade of burned brown to stick on a graham cracker that was already smooshed with a chocolate bar. I forgot about tomorrow's decisions and simply enjoyed the night.

And I enjoyed Jase, the good-looking guy I now worked for and I didn't even feel guilty knowing that I was greedily enjoying him because I'd learned while still in the cabin that he was a special person and good looks were only a part of that specialness. If I took advantage of that unique part of him, well if that was the case then I didn't care and I also decided that when guests came to the Center they could have his undivided attention but there weren't any guests at the

Center right now.

So I grabbed what special vibes I could get from Jase and squirmed a bit to get more comfortable and stuck my booted feet even closer to the fire, hoping the soles wouldn't burn while deciding that if I smelled burning rubber I'd withdraw them, but not before.

And I watched Jase. And I watched him some more. His profile in the firelight was the perfect masculine figure. Tallish, built like an athlete, which I suspected he was what with all the things that came with helping hordes of people enjoy the outdoors.

Could I do that profile justice in a second portrait? Should I even consider doing a second portrait? I'm not a portrait artist but I thought about it and decided that, since I'd always trusted my gut where art was concerned and because my gut had stood me in good stead in the past, I'd trust it this time too. I'd do a second portrait of Jase, one of dark and parkas and firelight on the night snow and it would be good.

I touched the snow. Just touched it. So white, so innocent, so soft, yet it had almost killed us both. I shivered and threw a handful into the air and then I watched in the firelight as it floated back to the earth.

CHAPTER 17

Minneapolis, when we arrived, was the same city I'd always known only now that sameness felt wrong because I was a different person than before our dangerous trek, a fact that impressed itself upon me more and more as our time in the city progressed and I chose which things to bring back to the Center – which was everything and I ended up ending my lease. Thank goodness Jase had a large truck.

Then we visited my parents, who had listened and cried when I called them from the Center to explain what happened but now turned white when they learned the details that I'd held back because they were scary and they wormed every single iota of the experience from me. Of course they did, they always could, but now I wished it was otherwise because they were shaken beyond belief.

"We had no idea."

"You should have told us everything over the phone." No I couldn't have, not without breaking down. But after telling and retelling what had happened, they said that the only important thing was that we were okay, and they still had a daughter.

We spent an evening with them and were invited to

stay overnight, with them insisting that they had plenty of bedrooms for everyone, which they did, but Jase and Petra were eager to get back to the Center. Petra's wife would be waiting. So we said our goodbyes and headed to the warm truck with my mom holding me back as we left the house.

She ran her fingers through my hair, comparing it to her lighter shade of red as she did when I was a child and then she gave me a peck on the cheek and turned to go back into the house because it was cold outside, really cold, but she stopped long enough to say, in a strangled voice, "I'm glad you both survived." Then she added, "Jase seems like a nice guy. You're doing the right thing in helping him."

My mom doesn't say much but when she does, it pays to listen, and her words made me feel better about the decision I'd made. Then, as she stepped from the cold outside into the warmth of the house where I'd grown up, she added, "After this, we'll keep in touch more often."

She shuddered. "Never again if we don't know what's going on will we let more than a day go by without calling." She shuddered again and then she stepped into that warmth and shut the door and Jase and Petra and I headed north to the forest and the Center, where we didn't even unload except for my paints that couldn't be in freezing temperatures, but rather we dropped Petra off at his house and when we reached the Center we tumbled out of the truck and into the warm great room because it was late and we'd had a busy day.

Jase made dinner. He looked me up and down, considered my tired expression, and informed me that he'd changed his mind about starting lessons on the

Center menu that evening so I'd know what we served and in what order. Considered me again, top to bottom and back before shaking his head. "It can wait."

He grilled hot dogs that we scarfed down and then we went to bed and I stared out the window at the night world that wasn't truly black because in a white, snow-covered world even night was only a kind of very dark gray and I wondered at the simplicity of that dinner.

Would simple hot dogs ever seem simple again instead of becoming the difference between starving and not? Would I ever be able to watch pantry supplies dwindle without panicking? I decided that perhaps that time would come. Eventually. And then I turned away from the window and slept.

The next morning, when I entered the kitchen the table was covered with neat rows of menus, each containing piles of recipes. Jase indicated one pile. "This is the Monday pile. It's what we serve on Mondays and in the coming days we might as well go through the whole week's worth of menus in turn so you can learn what we eat and how to prepare it."

I gulped, he relaxed and dropped the teacher stance and we proceeded to cook a normal breakfast of bacon and eggs, which was the first breakfast on the menu as it was served the first day a group arrived. As we ate, I asked, "Do groups ever stay more than one week?"

"Occasionally."

"Do you repeat this menu for the second week too?"

He divided the piles into two areas. The piles took up most of the table. "Most groups don't stay that long but the second pile of recipes is for those who do stay a second week." He picked one up. "If you'll notice, though, it's pretty much the same ingredients put together in a different way."

So practical. Jase knew his business. "To simplify purchasing and storage."

"Exactly. The stores in town know what I buy and they always have everything on hand." His eyes lit up. "Which was one reason I chose this particular event center to buy. Nice town. Nice people. Johns Falls should be proud of its merchants."

We had soup and sandwiches for lunch and Jase explained that guests made their own sandwiches from an assortment of ingredients but that he didn't want to put all that stuff out today for just two people so we rummaged in the refrigerator instead and, in so doing, I realized what all those plastic containers of sandwich ingredients were for. They'd be arranged on the counter for guests to choose from.

Much the same happened for dinner, though Jase did say what time to stick the prepared pot roast in the oven so it would be ready at precisely the right time. In fact, he jotted it down on the recipe itself, which said that never before had anyone but himself been the cook.

I considered the recipe cards. "This isn't so difficult." When the small pot roast was done that was a fraction of what would be cooked when large groups were present, I removed the huge apron that had been protecting my clothes while thinking how similar it was to the smock I wore while painting that also protected my clothes. Usually. Until I got so involved in what I was doing that I forgot and wiped my hands on my pants. Did Jase do the same while cooking?

I looked down at myself. There were grease spots on my shirt instead of the usual paint spots on my slacks. Jase, on the other hand, unlike what I'd imagined would happen when a man cooked, was immaculate which just shows that some people are born slobs. Me. My mother followed me around with a washcloth when I was young because she liked a clean house. It helped. Some.

"How's the cooking going? Not that you'll do it, I will, but you should know how it's done." He tilted his head in that way I'd already figured was typical of him and was one of the things that made him so likable.

"It's not so bad."

"Wait till something goes wrong." He grimaced. "Though, as I said, I promise to do as much of the inside stuff as possible. Probably all of it. This is just for information in case something happens, and you have to take over." Like if he fell and hurt his leg all over again and had to be rushed to the ER and I'd be left alone to deal with who-knew-how-many guests.

The thought almost gave me a panic attack.

He indicated the menus. "As you'll notice, the meals are the kind that can be kept warm for a long time because often guests are late getting back from wherever they've been." He pinned the menus and recipes to the huge bulletin board that covered half the wall above the table and informed me that it was time for me to learn my other duties. "The outside stuff. The nitty gritty. What you'll actually do."

I took a deep breath because this was the part I wasn't sure I could handle. But I reminded myself that I had to do it or, as Jase had hinted, the Center might have to close. I took another deep breath and followed him to the huge closet filled with all kinds of outdoor clothing where I'd hung everything warm that I'd brought from the cabin and from home in Minneapolis, plus all that my parents had added to the pile, which was considerable.

With embarrassed laughs they'd insisted that we take everything because they didn't want their only daughter getting cold at work, and they were making sure it wouldn't happen. "We didn't know what was going on and we'll never get over that lack of knowledge, but we're making sure Laurie will be as safe as possible from now on."

I'd already had a lesson on how to lead a snowmobile party when we retrieved the snowmobile that was broken down, so now Jase led the way to cross-country skis hanging on a wall in a small outbuilding near the edge of the forest. "Make sure everyone has the right gear in the right sizes and that they know how to use it and then load it all into the truck and head for the nearest groomed trail. Guests will follow in their own vehicles, so drive slowly.

"When you reach the trail, make sure everyone is correctly outfitted – and that's important because often they forget what they were just taught back at the Center – and then you simply lead them slowly along the trail much as you'll lead snowmobilers."

It seemed simple enough. It wasn't because Jase on crutches could ride behind me on a snowmobile but he couldn't accompany me on cross country skis. He couldn't even come with me to teach what to do because he'd have to use both legs.

"The Center advertises itself as ecologically aware so we don't blast our way through the forest but, rather, we go slowly and carefully." Good. That would make my job easier.

By the time we headed back to the Center I absolutely knew that I'd never figure out the right amount of effort required to keep warm while holding back enough energy to finish the course even though, on our trek to the Center, it hadn't been a problem. Knowing when to divest myself of extra layers had been instinctive.

Jase didn't think it should be a problem now. "It's like pulling a sled and you're good at that. Very good. Just remember how you did it. What you did. You set out at whatever pace you chose and as you walked you altered your speed according to what your body told you was right." He stared at his bum leg in frustration. "It's very similar."

I'd pulled a loaded sled from the dark of early morning to that same dark of night and I'd learned early in the journey how to pace myself. I looked Jase straight in the eye and counted the flecks of black in his irises and noticed with a mini shock that they were the color of the evening sky and said, "I will do it. I *can* do it." And, somehow, I knew that I could.

We did fun stuff the next day. I made snow angels pretty far behind the Center with Jase cheering me on. We chose the forest so as to leave the snow nearest the buildings pristine so future guests could make their angels nearby where everyone could see them. Jase insisted on making his own angels beside mine even though getting there was hard with crutches and making snow angels was even harder. I breathed a sigh of relief when he once again was upright and moving.

Next I rolled a snowball large enough to become the bottom third of a snowman and I did it in plain sight because Jase thought guests might appreciate having a start that they could add to.

Later, with Jase cheering me on, I slid down the hill not far from the main building on a sled much like the one Jase had ridden on our trip there. When I was done, I was covered in snow and laughing because I hadn't gone sledding since I was a kid.

When we went inside at the end of the day, I knew that I could do at least a passable job of the outdoor things that needed doing. Most of them, anyway. Maybe all of them.

Jase thought so too, it was in those evening sky eyes. "I'll keep the equipment working and in good condition. I can do that indoors and if there are any problems I can't handle, I'll call a mechanic."

"Could you fix everything if you weren't on crutches?"

"Mostly, yes, but some of it requires heavy lifting and I won't ask you to do it."

"I helped my dad fix cars."

He licked his lips so I knew that money was a consideration but in the end he shook his head. "Best not to take chances. I can't risk losing you and I don't want any problems while guests are using the equipment. Billy in town knows my machinery and will keep it running."

My relief was so great that I couldn't hide it and his not-quite-hidden smile said he understood.

That evening, as every day, we ate another small version of whatever would be served that day if there were guests present and Jase pointed to a calendar on the kitchen wall that I'd noticed but not paid any attention to. "It shows how many people will be here and when they'll come and when they'll leave to make sure we figure meals and portions correctly."

I looked it over. There were empty boxes on the calendar when the Center would be vacant, like now. I assumed that was normal for winter, which he'd said was the slow season. Looking at the filled spaces, I knew I'd be earning every free meal I'd be eating but there were enough blank spaces on the calendar to guarantee enough time to paint if I scheduled my time.

I suddenly wanted to finish the portrait of Jase I'd started at the cabin. The desire was a physical need, an itch that needed scratching. And I wanted to start on the second portrait, the one of him outside in the night with stars as a backdrop. I was itching just as badly to get going on that one and why I felt that way when I'd never done portraits before was something I couldn't fathom.

Was I changing, evolving as an artist and portraits would become my next phase? Or was it Jase himself? Was there something about the man that called to me and if so what was it about him that got to me so thoroughly that I wanted – needed -- to get that essence on canvas?

As if Jase could read my mind, he suddenly said, "I've been considering another activity that guests might like." He looked away so I knew this activity involved me, and then he looked back. "An indoor activity. If you're interested."

"Which would be?"

"Would you consider giving art lessons?"

My mouth dropped and he hastened to add, "If you want." As I managed to close my mouth, he went on. "You are an artist, after all." He gestured to the walls in the main room. The yards and yards of walls that were partly covered with woodsy decor, but mostly were bare. "And of course, as I said, you can display your paintings and sell them here. That would be wonderful for you and for the Center so I hope you will."

He grinned, seeing that he had my attention. "Lessons would give the guests something to do that's interesting and they just might decide to buy paintings by their teacher if they see them on the walls." He added, "Give it some thought."

"I don't have to think." The words came out. "I'll do it." Two pictures on that wall would be portraits of the Center owner. I could see them now in my mind and could hardly wait to get started.

CHAPTER 18

The first group arrived the next week in cars and trucks, some pulling trailers laden with snowmobiles, everyone laughing and eager for a week in the snow-filled forest. My heart sank as they approached, but Jase was cordial and confident and glossed over their concern about his crutches, gesturing towards me while relating how I'd saved both our lives by trekking through the forest and across a large, dangerous bog. A little thing like leading them on excursions in the wilderness would be child's play.

They believed him. I gulped and smiled until my face threatened to crack and wished I could die as I wondered what I'd got myself in for and what they'd do when they discovered I was a fraud.

They turned out to be nice people, mostly from Minneapolis and we even had some mutual acquaintances so that helped assuage the queasiness in my stomach when I first led those without snowmobiles to the cross-country ski trails.

Jase and I had already taken a group snowmobiling and it had gone well, but that trip hadn't been emotionally draining because Jase was behind me on the lead snowmobile. If anyone had had a problem, he'd have been able to talk me through what to do. Not this time. But nothing untoward happened and after we returned and my knees stopped shaking, I was glad I'd gone.

And so the week went, one day at a time. Jase's meals were oohed and ahhed over and three women were enchanted with a rudimentary, fun art lesson and said they'd come to the exhibit that would include my work in Minneapolis later that month.

I smiled and didn't expect them to show up but decided they were nice people and when the group pulled out at the end of the week, I felt a lift to my spirits that was both unexpected and exhilarating.

Jase and I waved goodbye from the huge front door, with Jase's arm casually around my shoulders. As the last truck with its snowmobile trailer disappeared around down the driveway, he asked, "What's this about your pictures being on display in Minneapolis?"

Oops. I'd forgotten to mention the show that had been scheduled long ago.

I studied his face. Was this a problem? His expression didn't say. "The gallery that sells my work has exhibits every so often. It's how they drum up interest and they sell a lot of pictures during and after shows."

"Do you have to be there?"

My heart sank. "Yes." And then, "I'm sorry. I forgot about it when I agreed to help here."

His lips pursed. "When is the exhibit?" I told him and his face cleared. "No one will be here that week." His arm tightened on my shoulder. "Thank goodness." Then he turned me towards the main room and dropped his arm to better navigate on crutches. "No conflict at all and you can take the truck because your car is still under a few feet of snow and I'm certainly not going to need it."

"Will you be okay alone?"

He snorted. "Just because I have a bum leg doesn't mean I need a nursemaid." He shoved me lightly and we went to the kitchen and had a meal of leftovers from the week, of which there were lots. "I often don't have to cook for many days after groups leave. I merely defrost what wasn't eaten."

He indicated the freezer with one crutch. The man was becoming a crutch expert. "Since all the left-overs were frozen in single portions, choose whatever you wish, and I'll do the same." So we each had different meals and dinner was wonderful and easy and then somehow we found ourselves in front of the fireplace that gave a winter wonderland ambience to the entire great room and was just as wonderful in its own way as the meal had been. I leaned back, relaxed, and let myself fall into a comfortable trance.

Until I felt that itch to paint and soundlessly got up and found my sketchbook in the room that was now my studio. I returned to the great room and began getting Jase and that fire down on paper. A third Jase portrait.

"Really? I'm not a model," was all he said but he stayed where he was so I could sketch, though I doubted he'd move anyway because he was totally relaxed and somnolent and appeared content right there in front of the fire. I suspected he'd stay there forever if possible.

The sketch went quickly and well. As the lines appeared like magic on the white paper, I wondered if portraits might be my thing after all, but in the back of my mind I suspected that it wasn't my ability as an artist as much as Jase himself that made the difference.

Not for the first time I wondered what it was about the man that made it so easy to get his essence on canvas and I determined to someday figure it out. Not tonight, of course, because tonight was for the fire and sketching and enjoying being alive in front of a fireplace in the north woods with a man who was – what? I didn't know except that he wasn't like anyone I'd ever known before and I couldn't figure out what was different but knew that something was. Something special.

All three sketches were finished in time to be included in the showing of my works and those of other artists in Minneapolis. I brought them, carefully wrapped, when I went to the city, having told my agent I had three pictures that weren't my usual type.

When I mentioned that they were portraits, he harrumphed and said I wasn't a portrait artist so, though he'd look them over and leave space on the walls for them to hang in glory if they were up to his standards, he'd also have other pictures ready to take those spaces if they were as bad as he expected them to be.

The portraits were included in the exhibition. Donaldo looked them over and then looked at me speculatively. He then walked straight to the wall and hung them himself instead of having an assistant do it, which was usual for him. I folded my arms across my chest and asked if he thought I had a future as a portrait artist.

I was surprised at his answer. "No. A thousand times, 'no'."

"Why not?" My mouth hung open. He'd gone

against routine, which meant they were good.

"These are anomalies. They are outliers." He shook his head in a way that left no room for argument. "They are good, I'll give you that, but they aren't your usual work, so don't stop painting the forest pictures that are your forte."

I forced my mouth shut. "You agree they are good." Unasked was the question of why they weren't an indication of my ability.

He rolled his eyes. Jase was across the room. He'd come after all and was staying with my parents and visiting friends during the exhibition. Wolf was happy with my dog-loving parents.

Now as Jase turned to see what we were saying, Donaldo realized that we had an audience and lowered his voice, which normally could boom across a football field without need of a microphone. He actually whispered. "These are not an indication of your ability. Rather they indicate your feelings for the subject."

"Oh." My mouth didn't drop open, but instead made a perfect circle. "It's Jase, isn't it? I agree there's something about him though I can't figure out what it is that makes him such a good subject." I glanced at the portraits that were next to my pictures of soaring evergreens and the mossy floor of the summer forest.

Jase's expression in those portraits said that if he walked the forest in the summer he'd know the exact places portrayed, which was possible because he, too, lived in the north woods. But there was more than that to whatever he brought to his portraits. "He could be a male model."

Donaldo shook his head in the violent way he has and gave me a pitying look. "It's not him. Not at all.

He's a normal male, there a million of him out there. He's nothing special."

"So what is it about him, then?"

"You're in love with him, that's what."

I froze, shocked, and couldn't say a word for a long time, until I managed to squeak, "That's ridiculous."

Donaldo shook his head pityingly. "Love. That's what I see in these portraits." He rolled his eyes for a second time and added, "I just hope this new obsession of yours doesn't send your talent into the basement."

He shuddered as if unable to understand how any artist worth his salt could be so inconsiderate of his largesse to them in helping them sell paintings as to jeopardize everything by falling in love. "I won't pull your pictures yet because you are talented and in time you may get over this infatuation. I certainly hope so."

His statement was followed by a huge indrawn breath that every worker in the room could hear and then he ignored me in favor of telling his current assistant what she was doing wrong. Donaldo goes through at least one assistant a month, that being the length of time they can take his harangues before quitting.

I just stood there and stared at the lineup of the three portraits, wondering if Donaldo was right and deciding, eventually, that of course he wasn't because, though Jase was a nice guy and a very competent Center manager, and there was something special about him in spite of what Donaldo believed and that something showed in portraits, in spite of all those things my feelings for him didn't rise to the level of love. Or even lust. Or anything more emotional than like.

Did they?

I jumped as Jase appeared at my elbow, whispering because Donaldo was close enough to hear otherwise. "How can you work with him?" He shook his head in wonderment at why I suffered through Donaldo's eccentricities. "He might as well have a horse whip."

"He's the only person who would look at my work when I started." Jase examined Donaldo and shook his head in disbelief. "He showed my pictures when no one else would and he has considerable clout in the Minneapolis art scene." Jase gave another shake of his head as we slipped away before Donaldo could corner us and say he'd heard every unflattering word. "He gives exhibits that are well attended, and I sell lots of pictures and that money enables me to be an independent artist who doesn't need a day job."

"Huh!" The single word said what Jase thought of Donaldo and then he thought long and hard and silently until he blurted out with, "What if you make our arrangement at the Center permanent? If I promise you time to paint in the summer when things get busy? If I pay you a small salary? So maybe you can cut your ties to this guy."

I twisted to look at Jase because his offer was so unexpected. "With free room and board and your paintings hanging in the great room so people buy them, then even if you don't sell as many pictures, you should sell enough to keep your independence and if you still want to connect with someone in the art world I bet there are other gallery owners in Minneapolis who will be happy to show your work now that you've proved your pictures sell."

He stopped for breath and looked away as he

continued. "The thing is, I'm getting used to having you at the Center. We work well together and business has been picking up enough lately that I've known for a while that I'll need help." He would have moved from one foot to the other if he'd been able, I could see it in his body language. "Well? I'm offering you a permanent job. Are you interested?" And then, "Say something. Answer me. Please."

I didn't expect to agree, especially not after hearing Donaldo say I was in love with Jase. Not that I was, but if it could in some incomprehensible way become true in the far distant future, then I should be running from Jase as fast as possible right now. Because more than one good artist has stopped painting when love called.

But as that thought went through my mind, a second thought countered it. If I wasn't in love with Jase – which I wasn't – then being with him day and night and working side by side with him would be the perfect way to prove to myself and to the world, Donaldo being the most important part of that world, that I was not in love. Not. Not. Not.

"Sure I'll work for you." I looked away just in case my expression told Jase what Donaldo had said. "I'll be happy to become a part of the Center as long as I still have time to paint." I raised my chin in what I hoped was a truculent manner. "And I'll hold you to that."

Jase put out a hand. "Agreed." And just like that I got a new job and he smiled in a way that said he'd been worried about my answer. "Now let's enjoy this show and not tell that agent of yours what we've decided until it's over and he's sold as many of your pictures as possible." He looked at the portraits and added, "Not likely to sell those." He shuddered.

"People aren't your thing."

In that he was wrong because the portraits were the first pictures to sell and they sold for more than the asking price when they became the objects of a bidding war between several art lovers who saw in them the same thing that I'd seen in Jase and they wanted that in their lives as much as I did. On their walls.

They fought each other and haggled over price until I was astonished at the final prices and when I calculated my cut of that price, I couldn't believe it. Neither could Jase, who couldn't imagine why anyone would want a picture of him in their living room.

CHAPTER 19

Back at the Center, Jase went straight to the bedroom that was now a studio and rummaged among my half-finished pictures. "We have a group coming from New York next week. You aren't taking your pictures out of that idiot's gallery until all sales from this show are final so maybe you can finish one or two of the ones you're working on here and get them hung before guests arrive. Let's them on the wall ASAP." He held up one that was almost done. "What do you think? Can this be finished in a week?"

I gulped at the speed with which my life was changing. "I think so. Yes, if I have even a little time each day to work on it." I flicked my glance to a couple more in similar stages of completion. "And those, also." I pointed. "If three isn't too many."

"This place has lots of wall space and they can be hung anywhere. Halls. Alcoves. Lots of places. Lots of pictures, as many as you can paint. We'll make them a part of the décor." I was awed. Jase was on a crusade and selling my pictures was the goal. No wonder gossip about the Center always mentioned how successful it was. The man was a force of nature.

We had whatever dinner was posted on the menu

for that day on the wall above the table. I'd already figured that Jase was slyly training me every second of every day and preparing meals in the proper order was part of that training, as were the seemingly random comments about how interesting it was to talk with guests so I should make the effort and what diverse people I was likely to meet and wasn't it nice that my horizons would become broadened after conversing with them? Which I surely would do. Converse with them.

All in all, I was impressed with the skill with which he managed his business as well as managing to integrate me into that business. Still, in private moments I was glad I was an artist and didn't have to worry about integrating anyone or about business of any kind though, as I reminded myself, since I was now part of that business, ignoring people was in my past. Learning to interact with them was my future. No more hermit lifestyle for me.

What had I got myself into?

When the group from New York arrived, I momentarily stopped breathing at the sheer number of people who'd be filling the guest suites upstairs. Under Jase's supervision, I'd changed all the linens and cleaned already clean rooms and left lavender sachets on pillows on top of evergreen sprigs that I'd clipped from nearby trees because, though he insisted he could do it himself, the crutches would have slowed him down considerably. I'd offered to do it alone and noticed that he didn't argue too hard.

I also filled huge vases in the main room with more evergreens. By the time those new guests who chose not to use the elevator trooped upstairs to their rooms, the entire place smelled of the outdoors in winter.

I wondered what it would smell like in the summer and realized I'd find out when the seasons changed. Flowers perhaps? Was there a flower garden for just such a purpose? I like gardening so I hoped so. In any case I'd find out in good time because I'd be here. I was a permanent employee as well as the first and only resident artist.

While waiting in line to check in, several guests had perused my paintings along with the other wall decorations, leaning close to check the prices. I'd held my breath and wondered if, when they left, one or more of my paintings would go with them. I could only hope.

A tallish, very thin woman with straight, cropped hair so black it had to be a dye job, called for someone named Paul to look at my picture of a very old evergreen that was leaning and ready to fall but was still standing, still alive, still fighting for its space in the forest. A slightly shorter, equally thin man with just as dark hair and a dark complexion who could be any of several nationalities, joined her and examined the picture critically.

I held my breath because something about his stance said he knew about art and I only breathed again when he nodded slightly and indicated the brush strokes that had showed the age of the evergreen and its struggle to stay alive while surrounded by younger, eager trees. He half smiled and the way he backed a bit said smiles were a rarity with him.

Then the lady pointed to the price tag and asked something. He leaned closer to see the price better and nodded. Yes, the picture was worth it. Then someone called them and they returned to the desk to complete their registrations.

When everyone was registered, I forgot the world of art in order to listen to Jase's quick lecture on what would happen during their stay because I'd be intimately involved in everything that happened outside. When he indicated sign-up sheets on a nearby table where those who were interested could sign up for various activities, I watched who signed up for what and how many names ended up on those sheets. I'd be leading those people through what Jase carefully called a slow tour through a winter wonderland and was exactly that as long as problems didn't arise.

The thin lady examined the potential activities with the same intensity she'd used on my pictures, though I suspected she didn't have a clue what the listed activities involved. As in what was a snowmobile anyway, and why would anyone ski across country when there were perfectly good slopes in Aspen and who over the age of ten played in the snow?

Something in the back of my mind tickled me as surely as if Jase had kicked me under the table and I strolled over to talk to her. "Any questions?"

She rolled her eyes and asked pretty much what I'd expected and I found myself talking her into a short cross country ski trip, which I realized would suit both of us, her because she didn't even know what she'd be doing and me because short was better than long. If things went wrong, we could simply walk back to the Center truck that would be parked at the entrance to the trail.

She called out to the dark-haired art expert. "Paul. Want to come with us? It might be fun."

Paul came over and signed his name in that script

that some artists develop that was recognizable as a signature but completely unreadable as a word and I knew without a doubt that she'd asked his opinion because he, like me, was a professional artist. I was proved right when he asked, "Who painted the pictures for sale everywhere?"

"Me."

His eyebrows rose. "You? Why show them here? Why not in a gallery?" The question was a challenge and I answered calmly that much of my work was in a gallery in Minneapolis but some were here because I lived and worked here.

He asked what gallery and when I told him, those thin black eyebrows rose a second time because the Donaldo Gallery was known even in New York, but all he said was, "Good for you," followed by, "Nice renditions of trees."

The next day I led both of them on a cross country ski trip along with two others who'd decided a short ski trip was an easy north woods experience. When we returned to the Center for hot chocolate and sandwiches that had been covered and kept fresh for when we came back famished, they all stated that it had been more fun than they'd expected and that the forest was beautiful and I relaxed and only then did I realize how stressed I'd been.

Paul sipped his hot chocolate in a way that said childish treats were beneath him so why was he enjoying it and then he chowed down on several sandwiches with another surprised expression that said he seldom ate so much at a meal but he was hungry after the exertion and so he was going to fill his belly. That expression that he failed to subdue completely also said that he was enjoying himself in spite of reservations about this unusual excursion to the middle of the country.

When he was full, he gave such a large sigh of contentment that his eyes went large with surprise that he was capable of such a bourgeoisie expression. And then, shaking his head slightly, he turned to me. And leaned close enough that no one else could hear. And said, "I like your pictures." And waited for me to respond.

It was one of those awful moments when I was supposed to talk like an artist and goodness knows I'm not good at that so I stared at him for a moment before gulping and saying, "Thanks."

His eyes rolled again, and I knew I'd blown it so there was now no possibility of anyone buying any of my pictures until he reached out and took my arm, gently drawing me from my chair. "Come. Tell me about those interesting forest pictures." Mesmerized by his look and the realization that he hadn't laughed at my ignorant words and left the room, I followed.

An hour later, I knew beyond doubt that if no one bought my pictures this time, someone would eventually because, according to Paul, they were good. Not great, I already knew that, but good enough to hang in anyone's house. Then he left to join a group before the roaring fire for a cutthroat game of cards.

As I watched him seat himself between a portly middle-aged man and a younger blonde woman, the thin woman with the dyed black hair passed behind him and trailed her hand lightly across his shoulders the way people sometimes do when they are claiming that person as a possession. The hair on the back of my neck rose. Were they a couple? Were they involved or was it just art? Had I made a faux pas when I spoke with Paul?

I wished I was intuitive about such things. But I'm not.

I turned to head back to the kitchen to clean up the mess from our sandwich lunch and found Jase leaning against the door, arms folded, staring at me and then at Paul. His eyebrows rose and he fought to keep from laughing as he moved aside so I could join him and finish cleaning what I discovered was an almost immaculate kitchen.

We sat down to coffee that reminded me of my father because it was from the grounds at the cabin and was even better than the hot chocolate we'd had moments earlier as he told me that I just might become a wealthy artist thanks to his decision to hang my pictures in the Center. His decision and his alone and he was taking all the credit for my future success. His eyebrows lifted in a superior expression and it was all I could do not to laugh.

But alone at last I hoped he was right while wishing he'd been bothered by Paul's attention to me, even though it wasn't romantic. At some level, I found myself wishing Jase had acted like a jealous lover instead of a businessman.

Why'd I care how he felt? There was no reason, none, for me to care whether Paul was interested in me or not because I wasn't in love with Jase. Donaldo was wrong about that. I wasn't in love or anything close. Definitely not. Surely the only reason for thinking such odd thoughts was because Donaldo had put the possibility into my mind, darn him anyway.

No other reason at all. None.

CHAPTER 20

The group from New York snowmobiled and skied and made snow angels and s'mores in a campfire after enjoying a picnic in the snow and then they packed up their things and returned to New York. After they left, I packed two painting carefully and took them to town and shipped them to New York where they would hang in the entry to the thin woman's penthouse apartment.

She hadn't said she lived in a penthouse, it was Paul who'd made sure I understood how wealthy she was and how important to the New York art scene. "Your little forest pictures will be seen by more than one gallery owner."

He'd then leaned towards me in the way I'd realized he'd chosen to do with me and me alone and I had no idea what it meant because I'd already figured out that he was different from anyone I'd known before and that I couldn't read him. Not at all. When he was done describing his wealthy friend, he'd added, "Who knows what will happen?"

He'd delicately backed up a couple of feet and looked me up and down and rolled his eyes a few times and said, "Too bad you don't do art-speak."

"What?"

Another eye roll. "You know. Art-speak. The language of all rich artists, me included."

"Are you talking about the things my agent wants me to say when people ask about my pictures?"

He'd laid a finger on my nose and smiled. Actually smiled. "Yes. Precisely. Art-speak. Your agent has your best interests at heart, as well as his own." He whirled away and trotted after the group that was headed upstairs to give their rooms one last look before leaving. "Take my advice, little Laurie. Learn art-speak."

As they left Jase stood in the doorway and waved goodbye to these guests as any good host would do. As Paul made an effort to say a special good-bye to me, including another mention of art-speak, Jase noticed and almost but not quite frowned and I wished it had developed into a real frown because that might mean that he was jealous.

Again, why did I care? Because I was in love with him? Of course not but as the rental cars disappeared around that first curve in the driveway I sternly forced any thoughts of Jase to the back of my mind and told them to stay there because I was sick and tired of staying awake nights trying to figure out whether Donaldo was right about me being in love with my boss. Partner. Friend. Whatever he was.

We returned to the main room and began straightening it up. Then we headed for the kitchen and checked the leftovers in the freezer that would become our next few meals, hopefully disguised with additional ingredients so as to seem different which was a real possibility because Jase was a genius at creating a million completely different meals from the same ingredients.

That day he made sloppy joes. They weren't on any menu on the bulletin board but were wonderful and made from leftovers that bore no resemblance to sloppy joes. He filled a bun and handed it to me. "Two pictures. You sold two pictures." There was awe in his voice. "I'm in the wrong business. I should have been an artist." He tilted his head in that unique way he had. "Except I have no artistic ability at all."

I giggled, still flying high from the fact that Paul's wealthy friend – the one that I suspected he cultivated because she could advance his career rather than because they were romantically involved – had bought two of my paintings. Two!

I enthused to Jase between bites. "She's going to talk to a gallery owner she knows. There's a show later this winter and she happens to know that at least one artist pulled out. She says there was an argument, which is pretty common in the art world. Anyway there's now space for someone else's pictures. Maybe mine."

Jase blew on his sloppy joe and then ate it in one gulp and sighed in contentment because he likes his own cooking. "I think that if Sylvia Ullerman tells the gallery owner that she thinks your paintings should be included, they will be."

He leaned across the table, sloppy joe sauce on the corner of his mouth. "That artist guy, Paul I think his name is." I stopped eating, my sloppy joe halfway to my mouth, and waited. "I think he likes you. Sort of. Maybe."

I examined Jase's face for any indication as to whether this bothered him or not while mentally castigating myself for caring. "Though whether it's because of your pictures or your red hair and green eyes, I can't decide."

He looked at me in a way he'd never done before, really looking, really seeing me. I felt his gaze clear to my toes and the warmth from his eyes spread over me like a blanket. "Too bad you can't paint yourself. You'd make a great model."

It took less than a day to clean the upstairs suites and get them ready for the next guests, who'd be arriving in a little over a week, but there wouldn't be as many as there had been from New York. Still, they'd find lavender and evergreens when they arrived. The north woods would be with them all day and night.

A small business from St. Paul was bringing employees to the Center for a few days of recreation during the day and instruction in the evenings. We moved the couches to one side and filled the center of the main room with large, folding tables with a screen on one wall and a smaller table against one wall near the kitchen for coffee and snacks. It looked very businesslike.

Later I didn't remember much about that group because, a week before they showed up and a bit more than a week after Sylvia Ullerman and her group had left, I got a call from her. Pleasantries took less than a minute. I'd noticed at the Center that she was phenomenal at cutting to the heart of any subject while being so diplomatic that her listeners thought they'd been chatting pleasantly forever. A real skill.

"Laurie, I hope you are willing to place some of your pictures in my friend's gallery for a show."

I gulped, took a deep breath and remembered how

to speak. "Of course."

"That's good, dear, because you're going to be getting a call from him."

We spoke a bit more but everything essential was said and just as diplomatically and just as quickly as she'd started the conversation she ended it and, I was sure, went on to whatever else was on her agenda for that day. I hoped that when evening arrived she felt good about her accomplishments because I certainly did.

I told Jase in a daze that I'd have to pack a bunch of pictures so the gallery owner could have enough to choose from. He nodded. "And you're going, of course."

"Me? Why?"

"Because you're the artist."

"I don't know anyone in New York. Besides, I don't talk art-speak." Then I had to explain what art-speak was and how important it could be to an artist's future and that it was an ability I lacked.

When he finished laughing and had wiped the resulting tears from his cheeks he said that between us we could come up with plane fare and a hotel for a few days and then he suggested that I might bring a few brochures for the Center along so we could call it a business expense for both my art business and for the Center. Lots of deductions.

Jase was always the businessman, I decided, and was glad because I'd finally figured out that it was his hardnosed business sense that had made the Center successful and that my paintings on the walls were an asset that had somehow snagged the attention of guests from half way across the country.

Not long after my conversation with Sylvia Ullerman and the subsequent one with the gallery owner who, just as she'd said, called and after a long, detailed phone conversation that required me to snap photos of every single picture on the Center's walls and a few unfinished ones in the bedroom/studio, it was decided that I should bring as many as possible because a second artist had cancelled and he had all kinds of space available. And because, though he didn't say so, Sylvia Ullerman wanted them there.

As I stuck my phone back in my pocket I wondered if there really had been two cancellations or whether, more likely, Sylvia Ullerman's money and influence had done their thing and he'd simply made space where there was none.

I shortly received a third call, this one from Paul. "I look forward to seeing you when you come." I didn't know what to say, how to interpret his words. "My works will also be in the exhibition, of course, so we'll both be there to talk with prospective buyers."

After a long pause, "Don't worry, little Laurie, I'll be beside you all the time and will kick you hard if you don't say the right thing and convince everyone that you're some kind of heretofore unknown genius." A chuckle at the other end was followed by, "Prepare to nurse bruises."

Jase heard all the calls, of course. The Center, though large, was mostly for guests. The spaces that Jase and I were normally found in were much smaller and we bumped into each other constantly. He kept quiet about the calls for as long as he could manage but he finally asked, "What were all those calls about, anyway? I know about the call from Sylvia Ullerman, of course, but you've been on the phone a lot and I suspect the people on the other end are New York types." His lips pursed. "Is everything okay?"

I told him about the phone calls, even the one from Paul. Especially the one from Paul, watching for any signs of jealousy but there were none. Darn. He nodded pleasantly and said, "Nice of him to mentor you. One artist to another."

I goaded Jase. "He didn't seem the mentor type when he was here."

"He was out of his element here. In New York it could be different, he'll be in home territory."

"I suppose so." Disappointment cascaded over me like rain. Jase wasn't even a tiny bit jealous. So did that mean that he wasn't the jealous type or that there was no reason for jealousy?

Probably the latter. So thinking I once again shoved those odd feelings that were pestering me and trying to come to the forefront of my mind back where they'd never see the light of day. No reason for such thoughts because I wasn't in love with Jase. Wasn't. Not even a little bit and if Donaldo read something in those portraits that wasn't there that was his problem. Not mine and I wished I'd get over my reaction to his statement sooner rather than later.

So thinking I whizzed through the next batch of guests and made reservations for a flight to New York and for my paintings to be shipped to the gallery and almost died when I found out what shipping cost and then I looked at the calendar one day and realized that it was time to head to Minneapolis and the airport.

My parents had already agreed to keep the Center truck at their house and deliver me to the airport and pick me up afterwards. They love me and are always available to help me advance my career even though they'll never understand how they ended up with a daughter who draws pictures for a living.

So one day I got on an airplane in Minneapolis and got off in New York and took a cab to a hotel where I spent an inordinately long time in an inordinately hot shower that did nothing to quell the knot forming in my stomach so large that it was impossible to either eat or sleep which meant I'd be a mess when I met Paul and Sylvia Ullerman and there was nothing that could be done about it.

CHAPTER 21

I figured out one thing as soon as I left the hotel for a jog around the block and a quick look at the city before heading to the gallery and that one glaring thing was that I didn't like New York. Nothing personal I said silently to everyone who passed without seeing me as I went around the block where the hotel was located while hoping not to be mugged or run over by the hordes of people hustling everywhere without seeing anyone, just their own reflections in the many store windows.

I decided right then and there that I don't like cities in general. I don't like the way the smell. Or the claustrophobia from so many extremely tall buildings that keep the real world hidden from view. Or the lack of flora and fauna. Too many bricks, I decided, too much concrete and not enough trees. I like trees.

While at the Center, Sylvia had mentioned that the trees of the north woods seemed to kind of resemble the buildings in cities. Both reached for the sky and blocked the view while being a kind of view in themselves.

I remembered our conversation and tried to see New York her way and failed completely. But then I'm from the forest and would have to change into someone else in order to paint those buildings, which I was sure was what Paul did on a daily basis, something that I realized was spot on when I finally reached the gallery and saw his works on the walls.

Buildings. Cities. Streets full of people. Night turned into day by a million artificial lights. What had he thought of my trees and ferns and moss and snow? Now those odd expressions I kept seeing on his face made sense.

Before I realized what was happening, Sylvia's arms were around me as she swept me towards a small, pedantic man with huge glasses in the middle of the gallery who was orchestrating a confusing mass of people and paintings. The whole thing added up to contained chaos. "Laurie!" Her arms were both protection and security in this strange place.

She turned me enough for the tiny man to see me better and then I got about two seconds of his attention before he nodded abruptly in acknowledgement of my existence and turned back to the total confusion that was the gallery being prepped for a show.

"He likes your work." The arm that was still around me propelled me towards a table with coffee and donuts. She poured herself a cup and indicated that I should, too. "Not as good as at the Center, but it's hot and strong." She blew on hers and gulped it down.

When the heat of the coffee had abated enough to allow her to speak, she said, "I'm having a few people over after the show. Please come." She handed me a card with her address. "Not that you need it. I'll have a cab pick you up."

She pinched my shoulder as I opened my mouth to

protest. "I don't want you to get lost. This isn't the forest, you know, where forest sprites like you navigate by the trees and whatever else it is that gets you where you're going. This is New York, it's a city, and it can be intimidating." The words 'city' and 'intimidating' were said with pure love. This woman belonged in the city as much as I didn't.

I belonged to the forest. The thought popped into my mind from nowhere and I didn't expect it. I loved the forest, of course but I'd always thought that love was much the way everyone loves a place that has been special in their lives. But to think that I belonged there as if I was a possession of the trees? The thought was both so ridiculous and so true that it brought me to a stop in the middle of that huge room.

Sylvia, however, gently propelled me through the gallery that was somehow and rather quickly, under the direction of the small man in the center of it all, coming together and becoming a place of art and beauty. Standing there, though, and moving where Sylvia indicated I thought about the forest and my place in it instead of the gallery. I realized the forest was where I should be instead of this place in a very large city of lights and traffic surrounded by way more people than I'm comfortable being near.

I stared at the gallery and the beautiful pictures hanging on the walls and waiting to be admired and purchased and I wished I was back in the forest. Or perhaps resting on the rug in front of the Center's huge fireplace with Jase beside me enjoying hot cocoa and s'mores.

Jase belonged at the Center as much as I belonged in the forest. He and the fireplace were made for each other. Thinking about the forest, about Jase, his face floated through my mind. The planes of his cheeks and the smoothness of his forehead.

Something odd happened. I felt an actual stab of physical pain and couldn't imagine why thinking of him would hurt. Until I realized the pain was because I missed him. Wanted to be with him. To hear that laugh that no one else could duplicate. To see him tilt his head and tell me something. Anything. Because when you are in love with someone, what they are saying isn't as important as hearing their voice.

Good Lord!

Donaldo was right after all.

I was in love with Jase.

As the realization hit me with the force of a cannonball I stopped midstride and Sylvia almost bumped into me but somehow she was sensitive enough to realize something was going on and so she said nothing, asked nothing, simply stood with her arms around me, protecting me from the hoards that could have run us over, as she waited until I moved again.

"New York is interesting but I belong somewhere else," I heard myself say and was glad I didn't say out loud that I wanted to be with the man I loved because that would have been embarrassing in the extreme but the thought was so new that I wouldn't have been surprised to hear myself blurt it out. Instead I cunningly said, "I want to be home."

"Of course you do, dear, and as soon as this show is done with and I've returned in some small measure the gracious hospitality that you and Jase showed me at the Center then that's where you shall be." Her gaze drifted to one of the huge windows that overlooked the city and all its lights. Love showed in her face, clear and true. "As for me, I'll visit your forests again, I'm sure, but this is where I belong just as you belong beneath a bunch of trees."

In a daze I followed her for a while and then returned to my hotel room. Somehow I lived through the show and smiled and smiled and smiled at all the positive comments on my work and of course I said all the wrong things but no one cared because I was a novelty, an artist from the forest who painted trees, of all things, and wasn't that interesting and doesn't she talk in the most charming way? Not like an artist at all.

I sold three paintings, all summer pictures containing wildlife and I wondered why no one wanted just trees and decided that perhaps city dwellers might not like them as much as I did but everyone loves fawns and wolf cubs and bear cubs.

I went to the gathering that Sylvia said would be a few people that resembled a mob scene where I enjoyed still another moment of fame as the artist who'd painted the pictures that now hung in her foyer and had been expertly lighted to bring out the subtle colors of the forest at dawn that I'd thought no one else would see much less understand.

She stood behind me as I examined them and said she'd had an interior decorator place them to best advantage and do the lighting and I finally knew that she truly appreciated the forest even though she was a city person. Then I drank way too much wine and was glad for the cab that took me back to my hotel room.

I sold still another painting to an elderly man who'd grown up in the Midwest and said it reminded him of a patch of woods at the edge of his family's farm and he and I somehow ended up in one of the many little places New York seems to specialize in that carry coffee every bit as good as my father's along with slices of multi-tiered cake that melted in my mouth.

Then I packed my things and couldn't wait to reach the airport and fly home. All during the flight, instead of the fleecy white clouds and blue sky beyond the window, I saw Jase and the Center and the forest we'd trekked through and I wondered what would happen when I got there now that I knew my former agent was right and I was in love with my boss and fellow survivor.

I wanted to curl up in my seat and disappear and was grateful that my seatmates were more interested in catching up on sleep than talking.

My parents met me at the airport and I spent the night at their house where I'd left the Center truck. The next morning as my mother made sausage and pancakes, she looked at me shrewdly and asked what was wrong and didn't believe for a moment my story of being tired from the trip.

I finally blurted out. "Is love always this bad?"

After a slight shock that she hid rather well, she gathered me in her arms while still managing to flip pancakes with precision. "It often is." She pulled back and looked at me. "This is recent, isn't it?" I nodded. "Let it age a bit, Laurie. Get used to how it feels." Then she tilted her head in much the same way as Jase. "Then, if you still feel that it's real and not going to disappear in the morning mist, do something about it."

"like what?"

"Whatever feels right. Walk away if he's married." I shook my head hard and her relief was evident. "Tell him how you feel if he doesn't tell you first."

"What if he doesn't love me?" He'd never said he did. Never acted like he did.

"Then figure out what to do next. If it's truly hopeless take a trip to the south seas and paint fish. Throw something at him because he's clearly insane not to be in love with you. Or simply smile and continue as always while you look for someone else to love." She let me go and piled the pancakes on the table and called my dad for breakfast. "Whatever feels right that's what you should do."

I wasn't hungry and couldn't imagine why I ate three stacks of pancakes before throwing my luggage in the back seat of the truck and heading to the Center to face whatever might happen when I saw Jase, knowing as I did that I was in love with him because, no matter what my mother said, I had to survive the immediate future while I was figuring out what that right thing she kept talking about actually was.

CHAPTER 22

What happened when I got back? On the surface, nothing. Absolutely nothing. Underneath, though, my world had shifted on its axis.

I pulled into the Center parking lot and Jase came out to greet me staying on the cleared area but using only one crutch because he was getting better. The single crutch was more for moral support than because it was needed.

He smiled and welcomed me home. A good start?

Then he hobbled to the door and opened it because I was carrying my luggage and, with a grimace, acknowledged that he couldn't yet help much. As I went through, though, his free hand grazed my hair.

A shock went through my entire body, electricity that made me jump and Jase quickly pulled his hand back and I couldn't tell him how much I wanted it to stay there because what would I have said next? That I loved him? The words would most likely scare him to death.

So I said nothing and simply let the moment pass and dragged my suitcase to my bedroom. But as I walked, I thought about that touch. That accidental touch. I took that mini-second gesture apart in my mind.

Was it truly accidental? Could it have been intentional? Was such a thing possible? Could it be that, miracle of miracles, he was in love with me? Or, if not in love, at least in the kind of 'like' mode that can lead to love?

I thought about it so much that I got a nasty headache even before my things were back in closets and drawers and even with all that thinking I was no wiser than before though I stared at myself in the mirror and gave myself a stern lecture on foolish thoughts.

I returned to the kitchen because Jase had mentioned dinner, rubbing my forehead and wishing life was as simple as when mere survival was at stake. Compared to being in love staying alive and getting us to the Center through a deadly winter forest had been easy.

Still as I entered the kitchen I realized that I was starved and maybe that had something to do with my headache. The smell of still another of Jase's gourmet meals drew me across the kitchen and into the tiny alcove with the huge table and the bulletin board. We ate and then went to bed as usual and I didn't fall asleep until almost morning.

Darn love anyway. It's hard on sleep. How could I continue? Would I die of insomnia?

I managed. The days flowed into one another as before I'd known I was in love. I adjusted and kept busy and tried to act normal and sometimes I actually succeeded. But I did notice one difference from before I went to New York.

One really odd thing. I wasn't the only one striving for normalcy. Jase, too, had changed.

He was different. It was hard to know exactly what that difference was but I finally figured it out. He'd forgotten how to smile and Jase, as I already knew, was the eternal optimist who saw the good side of everything and everyone and smiled even when the sun forgot to shine.

He wasn't actually unhappy. He didn't go around in a fog of despair but the smile that had come so easily and so often now appeared only on occasion and there were times – many times – that I caught him staring out the window or at a blank wall. Just staring.

At such times I'd call out and he'd start, look my way, color a bit and hobble off, swinging his crutch so fast I feared he'd take a header. And all the while he'd mutter something unintelligible.

He smiled when guests were present but my gut said it wasn't a genuine smile though no one else seemed to notice. At other times when he thought he was alone the smile disappeared completely and his mood could only be described as melancholy.

Other days his smile would return full force and rival the sun and I'd bask in its glory and we'd have such wonderful times that I'd go to bed giddy with happiness and hope.

I wanted to ask him what was going on but didn't because what if my question made things worse? Not to mention that I didn't trust myself. I'd probably ask how he was feeling and then spill out that I just happened to be in love with him and so was concerned for his welfare.

If that happened I was sure that being the nice guy that he is he'd say something guaranteed to make me feel good about being in love with him when he wasn't in love with me and then he'd get rid of me as fast as possible, never mind that he'd have to do everything alone.

So I said nothing. Did nothing. Tried to smile. Failed miserably. Was glad when my former agent in Minneapolis called. "What about another show?" Donaldo's voice was pure honey, which meant he wanted something.

"I thought we no longer had a contract."

I heard a ppffft as he blew through his nostrils, a ploy he uses when he wants something, which, together with the honeyed speech, meant this was important. "A contract is a mere technicality."

"Okay. So what do you want that has nothing to do with a contract?"

"I have a gallery and I want pictures to display in a show I've decided to put on to welcome spring and I happen to know that you have some fairly decent pictures of the spring forest. That's why I'm calling" He waited for that to sink in. "Unless you sold out in New York."

A joke. Artists almost never sell out, at least not until they are world famous or dead. "I sold a few."

"So you do have spring pictures." The honey in his voice thickened. "Want to sell a few more? Make some money? Get rich?" A slight pause was followed by another ppffft. "Pictures are meant to be seen."

"Yes, they are." Did I want to resume relations with Donaldo? Maybe if things with Jase got worse and they seemed to be headed that way.

"You are an artist, even if you don't know how to talk to potential buyers." A sigh. "I'll have someone follow you around so when you don't know what to say she'll say it for you."

I thought. Wondered if the Jase thing would work out or whether I should start looking beyond my life at the Center. Realized I didn't have a clue but our current emotional roller coaster didn't bode well. "When is the show?"

Donaldo sensed my mood. "Soon. Give people something to think about. Spring and buying spring pictures."

My thought grew. Take a break. Get away. See what it would be like living elsewhere. A practice run. Go somewhere else even if only to Minneapolis and Donaldo's gallery. "I'll think about it."

I talked to Jase, asking if the Center could function without me for another show and I wasn't sure if I should be happy or cry in my pillow because he didn't seem concerned with my leaving.

I was so desolated by his uncaring attitude that I brooded in my room and decided to do the show and stay with my parents long enough to think about my life. Afterwards maybe I'd still work at the Center. Maybe not.

Jase once again helped me get ready. We went from picture to picture on the walls of the Center and in the studio that used to be a bedroom. "It's a spring show, you say?" I nodded and Jase looked at them all with a critical eye before pointing to one of pink Lady Slippers in a tiny, secret glen. "That one for sure."

Eventually more pictures were chosen than I'd expected. I debated whether to invite him to the show and finally did because not doing so would be rude. "Will you come?" Wolf would be fine with a neighbor looking in on him. "There's no one booked for that weekend."

His forehead wrinkled. "Yes there is."

"There's nothing listed." I'd checked the reservation book and there was nothing on the bulletin board.

"This morning I got a call from a group. They come every year about this time. Most people come in the winter or the summer. Spring bookings are rare so I never turn them away."

"Should I stay?" It was my job, after all.

That smile appeared, the one that was now a rarity and he put aside that single crutch and walked across the room just to show that he could. Slowly but steadily. "I'll be fine." The smile didn't dim. "I know that all they truly want is privacy and solitude. No trips, no effort. So go to your show."

His words hit hard but his tone of voice said he meant it. He didn't need me. He didn't want me. Not at all.

That night I cried into my pillow because not being needed is horrid. Not being wanted is even worse. And it looked like both applied to me.

CHAPTER 23

What passes for spring in northern Minnesota arrived about the same time as the show. It took over the landscape, turning pristine, white snow into something that more closely resembled dirt while turning actual dirt into mud.

What had been snow drifts melted into small piles of snow streaked with brown and wherever the sun touched the ground for more than a few minutes green grass and weeds popped up sometimes through that very snow that was already sprinkled with bright yellow wildflowers. A typical north woods spring.

I love spring in the north woods and stopped crying into my pillow because no one could be completely unhappy with the lovely turn of the seasons, not even lovelorn wusses like me and I found myself looking forward to the upcoming show. To a break from wondering what was wrong with Jase because his roller coaster moods continued and probably had something to do with me. That depressing thought made me want to cry all over again even with the sun pouring down and tuning the world into a vision of golden mud.

Maybe I should just ask Jase what was going on.

I spent the better part of a week dithering like a

lovelorn maiden before coming up with what I hoped was a sneaky but valid approach. I spoke as we sat down to a breakfast that I'd made following the instructions on the wall and I'd only had to cut the portions ninety percent to reach the perfect amount for two people.

"I'm worried about you." A bald statement but it was a start.

"Huh?" He stopped eating. "Why? What did I do wrong?"

"Nothing. You didn't do anything wrong." So maybe it wasn't a good start after all but I plowed ahead anyway. "You're so moody lately that I'm concerned."

Jase managed not to speak for a long time by pretending to savor bacon and eggs, though I was sure he was beyond knowing what he was eating. So much for my culinary skill. "I'm fine." Another bite but he saw that his answer wasn't enough so he added, "Nothing's wrong."

Then he stared at me. Glowered would be a better word. "As a matter of fact, though, I've been worried about you." I pulled back in surprise. "Don't talk about me. Consider yourself. You're --- You're ---" He thought and then plowed ahead. "You're moody."

"Me?" No I wasn't. I was as relaxed as a limp rag. Except, of course, when Jase was around and then I'd get jumpy. Irritable. Unable to control my feelings. Because I was in love but wasn't about to admit it.

And, yes, there might have been a few times I'd dashed from the room to hide tears that threatened to appear because I didn't want Jase to see me cry especially as the crying was for no reason. But that didn't mean I was moody. Maybe a smidgen out of sorts but that was different than moody. Wasn't it?

Okay maybe it was the same thing. Maybe I was acting the same way that Jase was acting. Maybe we were both moody.

We finished the meal in silence, after which I shoved the dishes into the dishwasher while he stomped into the main room on legs that didn't seem to bother him at all in order to answer the phone that had chosen that moment to ring. When the dishwasher was going, and the call was done, he returned.

"We just got another reservation." He stared at the wall behind me. "Summer is filling up nicely." Then, in a neutral voice, "It's a good thing you're here. Even with my leg better the place is getting busier. It's getting known."

He continued, still staring at the wall. "I appreciate your help. Will appreciate it more in the summer when things really get busy."

He turned at last to look at me and we stared at each other until he waved an arm nowhere in particular. "If you stay, that is. If this work suits you." He glowered at no one. "You can leave, you know. If you wish."

Did he want out of our agreement? Was that behind his comment? Did he hope I wanted out too? I rubbed my forehead because another headache was starting. And then, horror of horror, I felt tears coming. Again.

I disappeared. I pretended to rush to my room on still another errand for the upcoming show looking out over the soggy world beyond the many windows of the Center as I ran and wondering whether we would be speaking to one another when that view was wrapped in summer green and the outside was full of people enjoying vacations as the birds in the nearby trees made nests and taught their young to fly.

How much longer could I not cry in his presence? I wasn't sure but somehow I managed until I left for the show. As I climbed into the truck Jase had the good manners to say goodbye. He even lingered in the doorway and waved and called a goodbye as I gunned the engine and headed out.

The warmth in his voice and the almost tragic expression in his eyes went straight to my heart and a few other parts of me that were lower down and ached just as much. Was his expression because I'd be gone? Or was he already dreading my return?

As I peeled onto the highway and made myself slow down before getting a speeding ticket, I wondered that I'd never known until then that a heartache was a real, physical thing. Like the wuss I decided I was I treasured that ache for the entire trip to Minneapolis. I wallowed in self-pity for a couple hundred miles and decided that a realistic future might consist of a million or so pity parties.

I reached the city and the Donaldo gallery and turned into the familiar parking lot as if it was an old friend, which, considering what was going on between Jase and me it might become once again if I quit my job at the Center and returned to my former life.

Donaldo loved my pictures. He said that misery must have matured me as an artist because I physically resembled a warmed-over, soggy, dead fish. He was probably right. "Get some makeup, Laurie. No one will buy anything with you looking like you lost the love of your life."

I winced and he noticed. "I've been sick." I coughed to prove how ill I was.

He harrumphed. "Lovesick." He sighed, sounding just like Paul. Was sighing an artist thing? "I recognize the symptoms as if those portraits you painted last winter hadn't already said it all." Another sigh as he helped lug my pictures inside. "I take it the love thing isn't going well, otherwise you'd be bouncing all over the place."

I didn't answer. His eyeroll was followed by, "Love. Oh the drama of it all. Sounds good until you consider the arguments, the shouting and flinging of objects and then the community property thing when you get a divorce. I'd never share my gallery with another person so love is not in the cards for me. Ever." But after he put the pictures away he tousled my hair in a way that was as close to sympathy as Donaldo is capable of before leaving to yell at one of his assistants.

The evening with my parents was much the same. My father asked if I was coming down with something while my mother, who knew what was wrong, clucked sympathetically and said nothing except vague statements about things working out for the best if you give them time.

Then I went to the room where I'd grown up and wished I was still that little girl with a paintbrush in her hand and a grand scheme for her life.

CHAPTER 24

The show went well as such things go. The young, blonde, overly eager and unpaid intern that Donaldo ordered to shadow me and take over whenever I threatened to kill a sale did her job well, cutting in numerous times with a toothy smile that charmed everyone and a spiel that made me resemble Monet. My pictures sold as well as those of the other artists and I learned that enough people knew who I was that I must be getting known in the Minneapolis art world.

I pasted on a smile and followed the intern about the room until I zoned out and the clock said it was time to close down so I could retreat to my parents' house and more questions by my father about what was wrong with me and more clucking by my mother.

I repeated that routine each day of the show.

On the last day I awoke near noon with time to shower, eat, and return to the show for the last, shorter day. The day that many people who'd dithered about whether to buy or not would return for a picture after which I'd pack up all the unsold paintings except those Donaldo thought might still sell because people had shown interest in them. Meanwhile I'd return to the Center and Jase.

In the shower as water poured over me, I failed to convince myself that things would be fine. I dressed carefully and went to the gallery and spent the afternoon following that overly-happy intern all over the place while wondering how my life had gone so completely off the rails and ignoring everyone who actually liked my work and wanted to buy something. Good thing the intern was there. Donaldo was a genius when he found her.

When the last of the buyers had left and the remaining coffee, wine and snacks were being devoured by the staff, Donaldo cornered me. "Dear Laurie." He sighed as if fatherly advice was not a job requirement and hard for him but he'd do it anyway. "Go home. Go back to the forest and that place you call the Center. Tell that man in the portrait how you feel."

He gave me a kindly look, something I didn't know he was capable of as he continued. "Give it time. Don't rush love. Maybe things will work out."

He shook his head as if wondering how he'd ended up in the supportive uncle role and said still more. "Go home and marry him and have babies or whatever it is that married people do. Just find time to paint a few pictures."

Then he gently turned away, took a glass of wine that one of the interns handed him, downed it in one gulp and sighed in sheer bliss as everyone pelted him with congratulations on a good show while I stumbled out into the fresh, spring air. It wasn't the north woods but there was a freshening breeze and I watched a rabbit scoot across the driveway chewing a sprig of green grass as it ran.

The next morning I slept in my childhood bed until

the sun forced me awake and then I packed my things, said goodbye to my parents, and swung by the gallery where the pictures that hadn't sold and weren't likely to sell were packed and waiting. Donaldo was there. On purpose?

"Think about something, Laurie." His face almost assumed its natural sarcasm but good intentions won out. "You have a job where you're in contact with the guy in the portrait all day, every day. That's huge. He can't avoid you and you can't run away from how you feel."

He scanned the horizon and stared at it for a moment as if wondering how he'd ever reached a place of caring. "I meant what I said yesterday. Don't rush life. Things might just work out the way you wish if you give love a chance." He shook his head aghast at saying such un-Donaldo things. "So give it time, Laurie. Give it time."

After some clucking and head-patting he reverted back to the Donaldo I'd always known gave one last very long shudder and retreated to the safety of the world of art that was his life. And his love.

During the drive home, I hardly noticed the early spring scenery for the scattered, errant thoughts that crashed through my mind and swept away awareness of the mud filled, thawing snow and crazy spring blossoms. Thoughts of Jase and me. Thoughts of a possible future. Thoughts of life and love. Thoughts of everything Donaldo had said.

Before I reached the edge of the big forest, I decided to take his advice. When I reached the Center, I'd take a deep breath, put on a smile, and pretend everything was normal and then I'd ask what needed to be done next because there was always something to do at the Center. I'd cry later in my own room. And while I was crying, I'd hope.

Of course with Jase's roller coaster moods who knew if my plan would work? I gripped the steering wheel hard and couldn't think what to do if, when I arrived, his sunshine smile was gone forever.

The sight of my tiny car in the parking lot blew all my plans to smithereens. My new life was busy enough that I'd forgotten about it. Of course even if I had remembered I had no idea what time of year the driveway to the cabin became navigable. We'd never gone there in the early spring. Maybe it wasn't usable until summer?

I parked beside my car and confronted Jase who was standing beside it and smiling happily with the old Jase smile.

"How'd my car get here? I didn't know the driveway was passable."

"It wasn't but I sweet-talked Maude into going ahead of me in her road grader to make sure it was safe and that wasn't easy, believe me, because she said it'd still be too muddy and we could both get bogged down and drown in mud and never be seen or heard from again. But I happen to know she's a marshmallow at heart so she did it and here I am and here's your car." He handed me the keys, grinning even harder.

That smile was capable of setting the woods on fire and as the following days came and went, I realized something odd. Something totally unexpected. His roller coaster moods were gone. No more moody Jase. The sunny person I'd come to know was back to stay.

How? Why? What had changed?

More importantly did the change bode good or bad for my future? Was he happy because he appreciated my help? Or because he'd decided to fire me and was just waiting for the right moment? Or didn't I figure in his thoughts at all?

Eventually, I found out.

It was a couple of weeks later when the snow was almost gone and the mud was drying and green grass was beginning to appear everywhere instead of in tiny clumps here and there and we were in a lazy mood that he'd assured me happened every spring because no one considered trudging through mud worth the cost of lodging so they didn't come and everything was ready for the coming summer season so we could do nothing. Absolutely nothing. We could be lazy.

It was evening and we'd remarked on how the days were getting longer. At last. We were in the main room of the Center after dinner with a fire roaring and coffee ready, the smell wafting through the huge place.

He poured himself a cup and spoke around it. "Tomorrow I want to take you for a walk on the trails through the Center's property." He added, "So you'll get to know them." As if making sure I didn't think there was an ulterior motive to his suggestion.

He put down his coffee and stretched until his hand grazed my shoulder. I kept still because I didn't want to scare him off and the shiver that casual gesture caused went through my entire body. "Believe it or not summer at the Center is quieter and more relaxed than winter because people come here mostly for a break from their hectic, noisy lives."

"What do they do while they're here?"

"Walk the trails, view the bog, and swim in the

lake." The tiny lake that I could finally see now that the ice was gone.

It sounded peaceful and lovely and I found myself itching to capture that tranquility on canvas. "Sounds nice."

"Tomorrow you'll see just how nice."

I stretched because I was still reeling from that accidental touch and couldn't sit still and somehow our arms got tangled until I brought mine back to my sides. "I love quiet summers." I did love them. I'd had a lifetime of peaceful summers at the cabin.

Later we put away the dirty dishes together and as I headed to my room his fingers grazed my shoulder. Then my arm. I looked to see if he wanted something and saw his mouth firm as if the tiny gesture had surprised him and had happened in spite of himself but he said nothing. It wasn't important. Then his arm dropped and I went on my way.

I thought about that touch. Maybe he didn't hate me after all. Maybe – just maybe – given enough time Donaldo's suggestion would work.

I crawled into bed and listened to the sound of croaking frogs that is part of spring in Minnesota and was glad I was following Donaldo's advice. The worst that could happen was that I'd end up an old maid artist with memories of years spent working beside my beloved without him knowing how I felt.

On the other hand, maybe – just maybe -- sometime in the far distant future Jase and I would be a couple. I decided that it wouldn't matter if it took months or even years because in the mean-time we'd be together every day of every week of every year.

So thinking, I rolled over, closed my eyes, and

slept the sleep of the just. And the hopeful. I awoke to a sun-filled day and stretched and tried to think what to do until I remembered that Jase had the day all planned. So I jumped up, showered quickly, and followed the scent of pancakes to the kitchen.

CHAPTER 25

The table was set, and Jase was whistling. I sat where he indicated and ate two stacks of pancakes with sides of sausage and orange juice. Then we set off to explore the outside portion of the Center after he filled a slow cooker with whatever we'd have for dinner. The man was methodical and organized, no doubt about it. He was also a good cook. I was lucky to have him in my life.

The morning passed in a pleasant haze of filtered sun as we strolled beneath evergreens along neat, gravel paths that meandered through just about every inch of the Center property without once crossing each other. Not quite a maze but close and the inconspicuous signs here and there told the untutored what they were seeing. White pines. Lady Slippers. A fox's burrow.

Then we sat without speaking on a bench just off the boardwalk that we'd climbed onto after crossing the bog during our life-and-death trek. No snow covered the bog now, neither was there ice and it teemed with life. A breeze sent scents both floral and musky our way. It was a special place. I could see guests spending hours on that very bench in silence. They'd come away revived and at peace with the world.

Jase surprised me with a picnic lunch from the backpack he wore. We ate sandwiches and drank pop on a cloth spread on the ground. The picnic ensemble was clearly Center property which told me that picnics were part of the Center's summer experience.

Jase must be giving me the full tour by treating me as if I was special just as he'd make guests feel special. He was making sure I experienced everything from the perspective of a guest which meant that he thought the experience was important enough to give this entire day over to just enjoying the best that the north woods has to offer.

We spent the afternoon wandering the shore of the tiny lake near the Center buildings. The water was icy so we didn't go wading but we followed a path that hugged the shore. I admired marsh marigolds in the mud of the shallows as Jase pointed out a bluebird house he'd erected that looked like it was about to become a family home.

By the time we returned to the Center it was late afternoon. The sun was sinking fast. Jase said that was the end of the tour so I could do whatever I wanted for a couple of hours until dinner. We'd have dinner in the large room, he informed me, in front of the fireplace where we could enjoy the fire and watch full night arrive through the branches of the huge evergreens beyond the windows.

I showered and took a nap, drowsy and relaxed as butter. As I toweled myself, I tried to guess what the future held. Today had been unique. A pleasant surprise. Tomorrow? I couldn't imagine.

What about Jase? What was his life becoming? When I left for the gallery his demeanor had been sour.

The smiling man of today was a different Jase, the Jase I'd come to know at the cabin. His special smile was back full and brilliant and I could only hope that it never left again and that smile was the last thing I remembered as I drifted to sleep.

When I awoke, I knew dinner was ready by the wonderful smells drifting through the halls and into my room. I checked the time. I wasn't late but I had no time to waste so I quickly brushed my hair and headed for the main room. The world beyond the Center was growing dark but the trees still were visible and a faint promise of moonlight touched the world.

I stepped into the main room. And stopped in total shock. And delight. The lights were off and a table had been dragged near the fireplace and set for two with elegant dinnerware I'd not seen before and candles. A fire in the fireplace plus those candles provided the only light in the huge room with the light of day fading quickly beyond the windows and silver moonlight growing bolder with each passing moment.

"Like it?" Jase was so close that I jumped.

"It's lovely," was all I could think to say. "Is this an extra treat for guests?"

I felt the breeze of the movement as he shook his head. "This isn't for guests. This is for us."

"Us?" My voice croaked. I had no idea what he was up to, whether it was good or bad but it must be important. It felt important. "Us? Really?" I actually looked around in case someone else had appeared to be included in that 'us.'

"Yep. Just us. You and me." He paused as the candles flickered and the fire flared and the last rays of daylight disappeared leaving a world of black velvet overlaid with silver. "Because it's a special occasion."

"What occasion?" Still croaking and no tact in my question, just a bald query, but I wanted to know. Had to know in case he was leading up to firing me and this elaborate scheme was merely to soften the blow.

He opened his mouth to speak but then changed his mind and shoved me gently towards the table where he uncovered a delicious meal. I'm sure it was delicious. It must have been to go with all the other preparations of the day. But I didn't see it, didn't taste it, didn't know what it was because I was in agony.

He finished his meal, poured us each a glass of wine and leaned across the table. The candlelight cast shadows across his face, etching the line of his cheek and darkening his hair and those eyes that had depths I'd never seen in anyone else. "First off, Laurie, let me say that I'm sorry. I owe you an apology."

I was unable to come up with a response because I still didn't know where this was going. Was this apology a prequel to being thanked for my help and sent on my way because I was no longer needed? Or something else?

"I know I've been difficult to live with lately." He paused and cleared his throat. "I'm sorry and I promise I'll do better in the future." Then, "But so have you been difficult."

I thought about his statements. Not great but it didn't sound like I was being fired after all. Not yet, anyway.

He went silent and I realized that it was my turn to speak. "That's okay. Something was bothering you but it wasn't any of my business and I'm sorry I was difficult."

"Yes it was your business."

I managed a tight laugh. "I thought it might be because of me."

"It was." Just as my difficult behavior was because of him.

I froze. Stopped breathing. My voice squeaked. "Because of me?" I dropped a napkin and cleared my throat and tried not to cry but tears welled so quickly that I wasn't sure I could hold them back. I blinked hard. "I'm sorry. Whatever I did to make you feel that way wasn't intentional."

His response was to rise and pull me up and over to the fireplace where he dropped to the rug and drew me down beside him. "Of course it wasn't. Because it wasn't anything you did." He grabbed a couple of roasting forks that he'd obviously made sure were available and slid marshmallows onto the tines of his. He handed me a fork and stuck his own in the fire. "Want some s'mores?"

I relaxed a bit. Not much but s'mores didn't indicate a horrid future. Even with the stress of not knowing what on earth was happening the fire was mesmerizing and no one can be truly upset while making s'mores. I put a marshmallow on my own stick and stuck it in the fire beside his.

The marshmallows were great. The day and the dinner had been wonderful. The fire was beautiful. But I still didn't know what was going on.

I wanted to know. Needed to know. Deserved to know. So I asked him, "Why are we here, Jase?"

There was a long pause. A really long pause. Then he said as simply as if he was mentioning the weather, "So I can ask you to marry me."

His words didn't register. I hadn't known what to expect and his proposal was so unexpected that I didn't realize what had just happened. "Really, Jase, tell me what I've done and I promise to ---"

Then the import of it hit. My mouth dropped open. My marshmallow fell off its stick into the fire where it joined Jase's because his, too, had burned to a crisp and was now a black cinder in the flames. "What did you say?" And then because I wanted to be sure, "Please repeat that."

He cleared his throat again. "I'm asking you to marry me." He set his fork down and rubbed the back of his neck. "I've been going quietly crazy these last few weeks trying to figure whether you have any feelings for me or not. The stress has turned me into a real grouch."

He carefully took my fork from my hand because it was dropping into the fire where it was turning red and would soon burn to a crisp and set it next to his. "While you were gone I did some thinking. I decided that the only thing to do – the only thing that could save my sanity and my good nature -- was to come right out and ask."

He cleared his throat again because he was having a hard time talking. "So that's what I'm doing. Asking you to marry me." And, after a moment. "So will you? Will you marry me?" Then, in a slight panic, "Laurie. Talk to me. Please."

My ability to speak had disappeared. Completely. I cleared my own throat much as he'd done and tried a few times to make a sound but all that came out was a croak. So, throwing caution to the winds I did the only thing I could think of to do.

I moved closer and threw my arms around him. As our bodies touched my stasis evaporated and I could speak. "Yes."

I thought about it. About my answer. Maybe my response was too tame. Too short. After all, he'd spent an entire day building up to this moment. The least I could do was utter more than one word. "Of course I'll marry you."

An improvement but I could do better. He deserved better. "I'll marry you with bells on. Wearing a parka. In the snow. In the spring. On the lawn. In front of the fireplace. Whenever. Wherever."

His sigh of relief reached the corners of that huge room and it was a while before we got back to the business of s'mores because suddenly there was much to talk about, and we were so busy learning about each other that s'mores were pretty much forgotten.

I already knew what he felt like. I'd helped when he was hurt and felt his rock-solid muscles but that night I learned more. I learned the slant of his lips when we kissed. How his arms felt when they were around me and how he felt in mine. It was an evening of exploration that lasted almost until sunup.

The next morning – actually the next afternoon because we went to bed so late that we both slept until way past noon – we called everyone and as soon as the weather was warm enough and the grass green enough and when his parents could come from Arizona we had a wedding. At the Center, of course, on the lawn and the weather cooperated but food was served in front of the fireplace that was already a part of my life. My future.

My father was much relieved to learn that my

recent illness wasn't physical and he was very happy to learn that the Center served decent coffee so he could visit any time without having to bring his own. He and my mother and Jase's parents spent hours getting to know one another.

Maude made sure the roads were smooth and the driveway in great shape and she brought her several grandchildren to enjoy the food and run all over the place.

I invited Donaldo and he came. His 'plus one' was his mother because, as he made sure I understood with a shudder of what might have been actual distaste, he didn't want to bring some blonde bimbo unpaid intern who might get ideas because it was a wedding and weddings made some women weird.

Eventually, they all left. We sighed, closed the door on the mess so we could ignore it, and turned to the business of getting started with our new life which didn't take as long as might be expected because we'd been practicing ever since I answered a midnight knock on the door of the cabin in the wilderness and found Jase on the other side.

THE END

Don't miss book one, The Pathfinder.

Dear Reader:

I hope you liked this book. If you did, I'll be forever grateful if you'll post a review on Amazon. Simply go to Amazon and type in *The Snow Queen* by Florence Witkop and then follow the prompts.

You also might like to read some of my other FGMN and TMA books so I've included a bit about each of them below along with a link to find each of them on Amazon.

And here's a link to my website in case you want to learn more about my journey as a professional author, about my other books and short stories, or my thoughts on writing fiction and on life in general.

http://www.FlorenceWitkop.com

Blessings and happy reading to you all.

Florence Witkop

ABOUT THE AUTHOR

Florence has been an elementary teacher, an IT person, has owned (with her husband and 5 kids) a family-friendly resort in northern Minnesota, and at present is helping make and sell fudge and fudge-filled treats, a family business she joined after her husband passed that started with the family recipe for Christmas fudge.

Most of all, though, Florence is a writer and has been ever since driving through near-blizzard conditions to the school where she taught first grade while thinking how she'd always intended to become a writer. Being a sensible person, when the school year ended, she said goodbye to teaching, became a full-time, professional writer and has never looked back.

She's been a ghost writer, written confession stories, done editing, written advertising copy, written some non-fiction articles, written literary and science-fiction short stories, written both novellas and novels, and won the only literary contest she ever entered, becoming Minnesota's Region 2 Literary Person of the Year.

She now writes for Winged Publications where she writes for both Forget Me Not Romances and Take Me Away Books. In this clean and Christian-oriented market, she writes romances peopled with happy, well-adjusted characters who aren't looking for love or adventure but find them anyway and the path to their happily-ever-after ending keeps readers involved until the very last page.

CHECK OUT SOME OF FLORENCE'S BOOKS HERE:

WILDERNESS WOMEN
The Pathfinder:

http://www.Amazon.com/dp/B07TLZFVHJ How long can a toddler lost in the wilderness survive once the temperature drops below freezing? How can a normally sedentary woman convince searchers that she—and she alone—can find the child before it's too late? Anna Reilly grew up in the wilderness and knows it like the back of her hand. Just because she's not a macho tomboy doesn't mean she can't make her way in the forest but she's away when three-year-old Bobby Deal goes missing and search parties are formed. When she returns, she's relegated to pouring coffee and handing out donuts. But she knows how to find the missing child if she can only get past the guards keeping throngs away from the forest lest they, too, become lost and make things worse. If only, somehow, she can get into the forest and start looking. She is determined to do her best to save Bobby's life and her chance comes when she sees Max Colton, her childhood friend who's stood up for her since they were kids. He's emerging from the forest to take a break from searching. With his help, she slips into the forest she knows so well and finds Bobby. But finding him is just the beginning. What happens next turns her life upside down.

The Healer: coming this summer!

TIME TRAVEL NOVELLA
The Man From Yesterday

http://www.Amazon.com/dp/B07NBL1XFZ What if you went for a walk and brought home a man from another era?

Impossible? Maybe not! When Carey finds an unconscious man among the wildflowers, he awakens knowing only her farm as it was a hundred years ago. He's clearly suffering from amnesia and 'something else' that the doctor doesn't understand. But when the doctor tells Carey that he'll recover his memories faster in familiar surroundings, she offers her home rather than sending him to an institution, not dreaming that he'll become a crucial part of both her business and her heart. But, as his memory returns, they realize the 'something else' is that he's actually from the past. He traveled in time. And may do so again.

JOHN'S FALLS ROMANCES
Shh – Don't Tell

http://www.amazon.com/dp/B077RMTT2C Recently jilted, Chloe Brown is back home in Johns Falls, Minnesota, working for her aunt selling furniture and other garden paraphernalia until she can recover emotionally, after which she'll leave. When she discovers a family of Mallard ducks in one of the huge vases in the outdoor portion of the store, her aunt agrees to let them stay because protecting the ducks is taking her niece out of her severe depression. Soon Chloe meets Ryan, short-term, interim manager of the Johns Falls newspaper. The two agree to support each other during this temporary, small-town stage of their lives, after which they will happily leave Johns Falls and each other. They find themselves sharing confidences, but Chloe has sworn to protect the duck family and keep them safe, so she keeps their existence a secret lest Ryan write about them in the paper, because a story could bring unwanted publicity, too many visitors, and possibly danger. But secrets have a way of being uncovered, especially by experienced reporters. And love isn't temporary.

A Very Black Cat

http://www.amazon.com/dp/B07BTGN58M Welcome to

Johns Falls, Minnesota, where everyone knows everything about everybody, often before they know it themselves. So it's not surprising that two people who are falling in love are the last to know, even though everyone's talking about their romance and asking them personally for the lurid, juicy details. (Of which there aren't any because this is a clean, fun romance.) But for the lovers to deny there's a romance even after being told straight out that they are in love? That's beyond belief. Meet Becky, dedicated small-town career girl following her pre-determined course to be the best bookkeeper in the area and now, with the blessings of her boss and all-around nice guy Tobias Whittaker, she'll also be a genuine business consultant with a framed diploma on the wall as soon as she finishes an online course that she'll fail without help from someone who understands the nuances of the people side of small town businesses. Enter Jackson, hunky, former football jock and newish, charismatic owner of the lumberyard in town whose charm can convince the must obstinate customer to buy something, whether that customer knew he wanted it or not, and whose boyish smile can subdue even the most stubborn heart but who can't keep his books straight no matter how hard he tries.

Add one small, black cat with a mind of its own into the mix that's not about to watch his two favorite people live without each other one second longer than necessary. Then, along with the entire town of Johns Falls, Minnesota, sit back and enjoy the action.

The Christmas House

http://www.Amazon.com/dp/B07H1ZYMSP *More than anything, Abby Carr wants to own the house in the forest where she spent many happy, childhood summers and she can have it if she follows the rules her grandmother laid out for owning it. Having quit her job and moved to the north woods of Minnesota to live there and eventually own the house in the forest, she moves in -- and realizes her grandmother wasn't specific about the requirements. Exactly what does 'living the old way' mean? And how can she 'make a living and become a permanent resident' when she can't find a job? But she'll do her best. Until, on her very first day she gets between a mother bear and its cubs and barely escapes with her life. Things go downhill from there and only the help of her hunky neighbor promises to get her through the year alive and undamaged. Bruce Merriweather grew up in the wilderness and pretty much knows everything there is to know about living in the forest and is willing to tutor Abby if she'll pay for the lessons with her to-die-for muffins, which he dearly loves. Muffins? Really? With no other options, she reluctantly agrees, ignoring his effect on her libido because both of them are too busy surviving in the forest to have time for romance. But romance has a way of sneaking into any and all hearts and Christmas in the forest is the perfect time and place for love.*

LEGENDS SERIES
Spirit Legend

http://www.Amazon.com/dp/B077TT5V53 Charlie, forester, guides her boss and the owner of Macallister Outdoors to a tiny lake in the middle of a wilderness tract he recently purchased so he can see with his own eyes the spirit that legend says lives there and uncover the truth about it. Suddenly, a rogue storm destroys the dam that created the lake, the surrounding forest, and much of their equipment. They are stranded. Then they see the spirit and hear it sing. It's real, it's beautiful, and it will die when the lake drains dry. They resolve to patch the dam and save the lake and the spirit. As they work, they learn about the spirit of legend and about each other, while deliberately ignoring the growing attraction between them, because a romance between boss and employee is always a bad thing. But some spirits can do more than just sing and look lovely. And romance has a way of developing even when it's not wanted.

Wolf Legend

http://www.amazon.com/dp/B077WCSBB3   Jane, who
dislikes wolves because they kill her livestock, takes Buck
Portman, wolf researcher and wildlife professor at a nearby
college she attends, to an island to seek out the huge wolves
of legend ... the dire wolves of prehistoric times ... that
local fishermen say they've seen there. She's skeptical until
a huge wolf runs through their camp and mentally connects
with Jane and invites her to visit so they can sort out this
strange mental phenomenon that neither of them
expected. Jane follows the wolf and Buck follows her into
another world, another dimension, one populated by larger-
than-life dangerous animals, including the wolves of legend.
Her mental connection to the alpha wolf is all that keeps
them alive in this dangerous world and when they return, at
the request of the alpha female, they take with them an
injured wolf pup to be healed. The pup heals nicely... but as
it grows, will it remain a pet or will it become a dangerous
predator in a world where it doesn't belong? As the
attraction between Jane and the professor grows, so do the
problems inherent in having a huge, prehistoric wolf in
today's world.

Earth Legend

http://www.amazon.com/dp/B077Y37FB8   Elle Olmstead
isn't your normal, every-day botanist. She's different. As a
descendant of Ceres, goddess of the harvest and fertility, she,
like others of her family, has a magic touch with plants.
Real, honest-to-goodness magic. Which is why she
unwillingly stows away on the Destiny, a space ship filled
with ten thousand colonists heading for a distant planet.
Because she knows that her abilities are essential to keep the
plants alive that keep the colonists alive and that will be the
basis for their survival when they reach their destination.
She's caught and thrown in prison, where her powers are
useless. Soon the plants begin to shrivel and die. Starvation

is imminent, not to mention that the plants provide essential oxygen. But no one believes her when she tells them who she is and what she can do, especially not Cullen Vail, the one person she has come to like, maybe even love. Because Cullen is head of Security, an inscrutable, military type who has no time for stowaways and doesn't believe in foolish legends. She lied before, why should he believe her now? But somehow she must persuade him of the truth or ten thousand people will die.